The WRECKERS

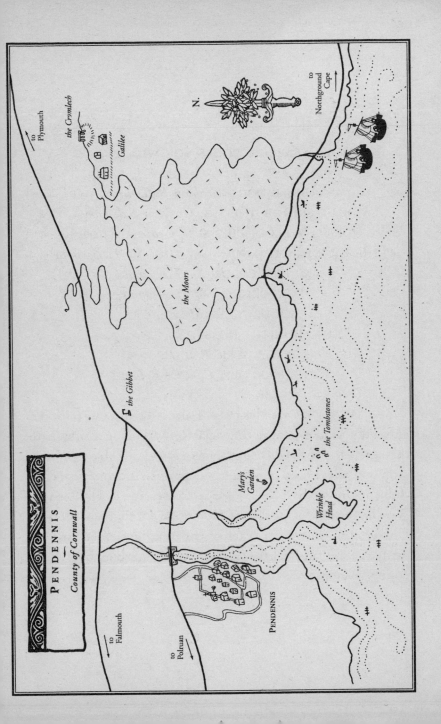

The WRECKERS

Iain Lawrence

A Yearling Book

Published by
~~Bantam Doubleday Dell Books for Young Readers~~
a division of
Random House, Inc.
1540 Broadway
New York, New York 10036

Visit us on the Web! www.randomhouse.com

Educators and librarians, for a variety of teaching tools, visit us at www.randomhouse.com/teachers

ISBN: 0-440-41545-4

Reprinted by arrangement with Delacorte Press
Map by Virginia Norey

Printed in the United States of America

December 1999

10 9 8 7 6 5 4 3 2 1

OPM

For my father

CONTENTS

The WRECKERS

Chapter 1
THE WRECK

For seven days we ran before the storm. We raced through waves that seemed enormous, chased by a shrieking wind. We ran toward England under topsails and jib, in a brig called the *Isle of Skye*. She leaked from every seam, from every hatch and skylight. But she went like a witch mile after mile, wrapped in a shroud of spray.

I was wet and cold, and sometimes frightened. But I loved it all, my first time at sea.

Skye was my father's ship, though he was never a sailor. To him, the sea was a nuisance, and the ship was a thing to be owned, like his carriage and his office desk. "Only owners and admirals," he liked to boast, "can order a captain about." And this rare voyage—Father had called it a ride—was meant to teach me that a scribbling of ledgers was better than a life at sea. "You want to be a sailor?" he'd said. "Why, you'd be driven mad by the boredom."

1

And he'd laughed. "Or scared out of your wits. So it's one and the same."

But I was never at loose ends, and not once so scared as that. We'd filled the ship with Italian linen and Turkish raisins, and with Spanish wine that we'd loaded on a strange and mysterious night. We'd covered the deck with chicken coops, and then sailed for home. And on the seventh night of our return trip, the barometer was rising.

The cautious little crosses on Captain Stafford's chart showed us seven leagues southwest of Plymouth. But even that was too close to land, and Stafford begged my father to let him heave to until daybreak. "I'm not at all sure where we are," he said.

Father would have none of it. "Raisins," he said, shaking a finger. "Raisins don't keep well in salt air."

So on we went. And an hour before dawn, the *Isle of Skye* hurtled down a wave. She hit the trough in a burst of spray, and water filled the deck. A thousand times we'd done that, and might a thousand more, but now the chickens rose from their perches and hurled themselves, shrieking, against the cages. An old sailor named Finnigan Quick stared at them with horror.

"Land," he said. "They smell the land!"

My father was beside me, his hand clutching a backstay, his scarlet cape flapping in the wind. He lowered his head against the spindrift, then grabbed my collar. His golden ring was cold as ice, and it pressed against my neck as he pulled me right against him.

"Go below," he said. His beard was like hoarfrost on my cheek. "Go, John. You'll not be scared down there."

"But I'm not scared up here," I said. "We're fetching the shore, and—"

He gave me a push, to send me on my way. But I didn't go below; for the first time in all my fourteen years, I disobeyed my father. I climbed to the weather shrouds and hooked myself to them like a spider. And the next wave rolled us over so far that I was lying flat above the sea.

It seemed forever until the ship found her feet again. And then the lookout cried down from the maintop, his voice made ghostly by his speaking trumpet. "Land ho! Land ho!"

He was invisible up there, where the storm clouds tangled in the rigging. It might have been God Himself who hailed us from the heavens.

"Breakers ahead!"

I saw my father stiffen. He looked frightened and lost, like a deer about to flee. At the wheel, the helmsman wrestled with the ship. But Father didn't move, and others came running past him. There was Cridge, the mate, his white hair blowing like a horse's mane. Danny Riggins was beside him, the foretopman from Plymouth. They threw their weight on the wheel and brought the brig to her course. And up from the ship's waist in his dark tarry-breeks came the master.

"Captain Stafford!" cried my father. He clutched at the man's arm.

Stafford shook him off. "Up helm," he shouted. "Up helm and wear ship!"

It might have torn the masts out of her. But the *Isle of Skye* was a good strong ship, and she flung herself round

3

on a crest. The yards went over with a squeal of blocks. From stem to stern she shivered. Then the wind slammed against her, and she heeled so far that the mainsail yard tore a furrow from the water. Down below, something snapped with a gunshot sound, and I heard the rumble of barrels as the cargo came loose.

. A wave as high as the maintop shattered on the weather side and pushed the brig down in the trough. I was under water one moment, then gasping for air, then under again. I heard a man scream, high and shrill.

And after it came the sound of the breakers. It was a thrumming, throbbing noise. It was a low pulse, like a heart-beat. My father's head came up, turning like a hawk's. And suddenly, like a thunderclap, the mizzen topsail shredded into rags and rope.

The *Isle of Skye* came upright, then settled again with the scuppers in the sea, water tumbling over the rail.

"As you bear," yelled Captain Stafford. He raised his head, his hands cupped round his mouth. "Masthead there," he screamed.

But the lookout had disappeared.

A man came aft with a dripping wet rag in his hands. "The pumps," he said. "They're clogged with something."

"With what?" said Stafford.

"Sawdust, I think." He shook out his rag, and a flurry of red-colored shavings scattered to the deck.

Father gazed at them with something like horror. Only later would I learn what he saw in those shavings, what terrible message was written in the sawdust. At the time, I thought only of the pumps.

"Can you clear them?" asked Stafford.

"We'll try." The rag was the man's cap. He wrung it out and put it on as he staggered forward again.

The ship hurtled on. Spray swept over the deck like a series of rainstorms, blinding the men at the helm. But above them, in the shrouds, I could see the shoreline and the glimmer of breaking waves.

And then the lights.

There were two of them, one above the other, like golden eyes shining in the darkness. I sprang from the shrouds and raced down the deck. "Lights," I cried, and tugged my father's billowing cape. "Lights."

He was angry at first, furious to see me. Then he understood, and he grabbed my arm. "Where?" he said.

"There!"

He sighted along my arm, and Stafford did the same. The brig rose from a trough, and the lights were nearly dead ahead. Then a third appeared, tossed by the wind, as though from the mast of a ship.

The captain frowned. "Now what the devil is all this?"

"A beacon," said Father. He laughed. "A harbor."

"Maybe," said Stafford. "But which one?"

"Plymouth!" Father cried.

Riggins stomped up the slope of the deck. He winked at me, then put a huge hand on his beard and squeezed out half a pint of water. "T'aint Plymouth," he said. "I was born and raised thereabouts, and I'll tell you that much. T'aint Portloe neither, nor Salcombe nor Fowey."

"Damn your eyes!" my father roared. "What does it matter where it isn't?"

5

Poor Riggins reared back as though Father had hit him. "It's nowhere, is what I mean," he mumbled. "Nowheres I know."

My father gave him an awful stare, full of fear and anger. In London he would never have raised his voice like that, not to the lowest of clerks. The wind swirled his cape around him.

"Make for the harbor," he said.

Captain Stafford touched his arm. "We'll have daylight in an hour, Mr. Spencer. We could stand off and wait—"

"Or sink like a stone," said Father. "We've got torn sails and a bilge full of water and no pumps to lift it out. And now we've got a beacon to guide us."

"I don't like it," said Stafford. A sheet of spray hurled against us. "I haven't liked this voyage from the start. Loading cargo in the dead of night. Skulking like thieves. I don't know what you're up to, Mr. Spencer, but—"

"Watch your tongue!" snapped Father. We were making leeway by the second. The sound of surf rolled like giant drums, louder and louder still. "This is *my* ship, and you'll do as I say. Now, I'm telling you to take it in."

Stafford turned away. He wasn't happy, but he would do it. He put his hands to his mouth and shouted his orders. "Hands to sail stations! Square to the wind!" The helmsmen cranked the wheel around, hand over hand on the spokes.

"Wear-O!" yelled Stafford.

The *Isle of Skye* swung quickly round until her gaunt finger of a bowsprit pointed straight at the beacons.

Riggins frowned. Then he saw me watching, and fixed a

6

smile in place. He always had a smile for me, though never before so grim as that.

"Aloft with you, John," said Stafford. "You're our eyes now."

I watched those lights as though they marked the gates of heaven. I stared so hard that my eyes ached. And when the uppermost light seemed to slide off to one side, I cupped my hands to my mouth and shouted at the helm. "Starboard!"

The bowsprit jogged across the clouds. "Steady as you go!" I sang out.

Cridge peered at the compass and scratched his wooly head.

The band of surf swept closer, a headland jutting out. We flashed past it and reeled on toward the beacons, across a bay where fires burned along the shore. Then, as I watched, the lights parted, though the brig had strayed not at all from her course.

"This isn't right," said Cridge.

We heard the beat of surf again, but from ahead this time. And a different sound now, a rumbling avalanche that grew louder by the moment.

And then I saw it, we all did, a patch of sea turned white by foam and spindrift. The waves broke on jagged slabs of rock roaring and bursting high in spouts of spray.

"The Tombstones," cried Riggins. "God save us! We're on the Tombstones."

"Put the helm down," the captain shouted. "Luff up or she's lost!"

The brig rolled as the bowsprit swung below the beacons. In the eerie glow of a burning dawn I saw figures up along the clifftop, and a line of land that almost ringed our little ship. She was turning quickly, rounding up to the wind. And she was almost at the eye when she struck the rocks with a jolt that knocked me from the shrouds.

The ship bounced free, then struck again, so hard the topmast broke. It toppled slowly at first, then hurtled down in a tangle of rigging. The wheel spun madly.

The first wave crashed broadside into the ship, flinging chunks of rail high into the rigging. The second carried away the longboat and shattered the windows of the stern cabin. The poor *Isle of Skye* groaned like a living thing.

My father, up to his knees in water, struggled toward me with his hands held out before him. The third wave fell across us, and dragged me down the deck. I reached up. "Help me," I said. I couldn't swim. Then I was tumbling down in a cold black wave, sucked backward to the sea.

Chapter 2
A DROWNING

The sand was cold against my cheek, and gritty. It felt a bit like my father's beard, and I suppose I'd been dreaming of him when I came awake. I was lying on my side, high up the beach, and the ground shook from the surf that hammered down along the shore. It was full daylight, but gray and somber, and I had no idea how much time had passed. It hurt to move, to even breathe — my throat was burning from seawater. But I pushed myself up on one elbow and looked round.

The sky was filled with gulls. They soared in huge, lazy circles, overlapping like the wheels and cogs of an engine. There were scores of them, all crying as they dipped and twirled.

I was nestled in a mass of bull kelp, the thick cords slick and wet against my bare arms. And when I shifted, they went slithering over my skin like giant eels. My jacket had been torn away, and two slats from a chicken coop were

9

bound on my wrist like a flimsy manacle. There were scraps of wood all round, and heaps of barrel staves from our cargo of wine.

The beach formed a half circle of glistening sand, a cove broken by reefs and backed by precipitous cliffs. I lay just above the water and just behind a rocky ledge that broke the surf along my bit of shore. Behind it, in an arc along the beach, the combers rolled in—lines of pale green water with streaks of sand in them. And beyond that, the hull of the *Isle of Skye* lay upon a shelf of twisted rocks that jutted up like rows of gravestones.

It was an awful sight to wake up to. The masts were broken stumps, the deck a shattered ruin. Half the planks had been torn from the hull, and in places I could see right through the ribs to the insides of the ship. My father's cabin lay split apart, his ledgers and books spilling from the table, his chest and chairs and carpets heaped against the hull. The deckhouse was gone, or most of it, and the brig's massive bones stood above the bay like the skeleton of a rotting whale, black against the sky. On the lee side, topmasts, yards, and bowsprit drifted alongside the wreck in a snarl of rigging. Barrels bobbed all across the bay.

In the surf a cable's length away, a body rolled in the waves. He wore seamen's clothes, striped and patched; his hair was pigtailed and tarred. As each wave came in, the dead man rose up the beach, then slipped away, tumbling down the sand. Then he turned and lay supine, fixing me with a horrid, toothy grin.

It was a sailor I'd known as Tom, and he'd taught me how to splice. His fingers, strong as marline spikes, now were bent and swollen. When the next breaker came in, up he went again, arms waving as though he were beckoning me to join him. Many times I had sat with Tom, but now I shuddered and turned away.

There were other bodies in the sand, scattered here and there, each a dark and huddled shape that was once a friend of mine.

And then I saw the men, across the bay, three of them coming toward me. They wore coats with big shoulder capes that flew about them like battle flags. They were kicking at the wreckage, bending down sometimes to pick up bits of flotsam, nudging at the bodies as though looking for survivors. And above them, the seagulls circled like a swirling cloud.

I tried calling out, but only a gurgle came from my throat, a strangled sound and a dribble of water. But they were coming to help, if I would only lie and wait. And I watched as they paced along the beach in a ragged, wind-blown line. They stopped at the body of a sailor lying sprawled on the sand. One of the caped men—he had a black beard square as a shovel blade—bent down and raised the head by its tousle of hair. I swallowed and coughed, and tried again to shout.

"This one's dead," said the bearded man. He opened his fingers and let the head drop back to the sand. "Is that the lot of 'em, then?"

I tugged and pulled at the kelp. I kicked at it, afraid they would pass me by.

One of the men pointed. He shouted, "There's another." But instead of coming toward me, they angled off to the water's edge, down to a sheltered pool behind a reef of jagged rock. A sailor lay there, not quite ashore but not quite afloat, one hand fixed like a claw to a clutch of mussels. When he raised his head I saw it was old Cridge with his white hair plastered down, his eyes swollen and red. He hadn't the strength to pull himself from the sea—he could barely hold his mouth above it—and his legs swung to and fro in the surge of water.

The men waded in, their big seaboots kicking up white froth, their coats streaming back, the oilskin thrumming in the wind like slack jibs. They stood in an arc round him, their hands on their hips. When Cridge looked up at them I saw on his face an expression of utter, wretched fear. And then the man in the middle raised his boot and set it down on Cridge's head. He did it slowly, deliberately; he put his heel on the crown of the mate's head, and pushed it under the water.

I wanted to cry out, but dared not. These men weren't rescuers. They hadn't come to save us, but to kill us. And I could only watch as Cridge's hand came free from the mussels, came groping up to claw at the man's rolled-down boot top. His other hand swept up, streaming water, and clutched on beside it. His legs thrashed and kicked.

But the man didn't move. He only stood there and put more of his weight on that foot, and the water bubbled around his boot through a mat of snowy hair. Old Cridge flailed and splashed in the shallow pool, his motions growing frantic, and then subsiding. But the man paid the drowning sailor no more attention than he'd give to a dog pawing at his foot. He took a pipe from his pocket, tamped the bowl with his thumb, and then shook the stem toward the wreck of the *Isle of Skye*.

"Right square on the Tombstones," said he. "Bad bit of luck there."

"We brought her in, Caleb," said the man on his right.

"Oh, we did that. But half a cable on either side, and she'd be lying high and dry, and there for the picking." Then he clucked and spat, and the caped men stood ragged in the wind, their backs toward me, staring at the wreck.

In a flash I was up. I shook off the last tangles of kelp, cast away the slats from my wrist. I took a step back, another. One of Cridge's hands slid down the man's boot, and I saw the fingernails torn away, the smears of blood they left on the oiled leather. The man they called Caleb pressed harder, but with no more thought or care. He just pushed with his boot as he shook his pipe and talked.

"Still, with this sea running, she'll be down to splinters and chips by nightfall," he said. "Won't be nothing left but the ballast stones."

I turned and ran. It was no more than five yards to the rocks, but it seemed a mile. My boots sank in the sand. I stumbled, caught myself, stumbled again. I kicked at the sand, grabbed at it; I half crawled and half ran. At every moment I expected a shout behind me, a cry of alarm. And then I was up among the rocks, into a crevice at the cliffs, and when I looked back the men were still standing in the shallows. Poor old Cridge floated at their feet like a straw man. Then I saw with dread the tracks that I'd left, the marks, as though a whole regiment had fled along the beach. And without a second's pause, I turned and tackled the cliff.

The rocks were slick with rain and spray. Three times I nearly fell; twice I hung by my fingertips from bare nubs of stone, my feet swinging in air sixty feet above the sand. Once I sent a little spray of pebbles skittering down, and pressed myself against the rock, waiting for that shout from below.

As I climbed, the bay opened below me. I saw the fires, still burning, women gathered around them in billowing shawls. Where a rutted track emerged from the gully, wagons were drawn up on the sand, wild-haired ponies standing in slack harness. Men labored back and forth, carrying boxes and barrels and armfuls of wood, staggering back-bent under piles of linens and clothes. One hauled up a sailor's sea chest over his shoulder. Another dragged a long snake of rope. They dropped their things in haphazard piles, and at each stack a child sat guarding the treasures, as though these men who plundered the wreck might also steal from each other.

Then I reached up my hand and felt, not rock, but a warm stubble of grass. And I pulled myself to the top, and crouched on a narrow ridge. It dropped nearly as steeply on the other side, down to a harbor and a little village on its far shore. The buildings there were whitewashed, roofed with thatch or with copper turned green by the salt air. A cart went weaving up a narrow lane, and beside it, with her load of sticks, walked a woman in ivory shawls. Boats lay dry on the tide, each reflected in the shallows of a river that came down under a bridge of arched stone. On the hill above the village stood a church. There was safety there, and rescue, if only I could reach it.

The wind pulled me and pushed me; it swept like a scythe through the yellowed grass and on from there — forever, it seemed — across a desolate moor. Wave after wave of low, barren hills marched to the sky, and not a single tree stood among them. Yet a pair of ponies grazed just a hundred yards from the clifftop, hobbled and heads down.

I took a step toward them. They lifted their heads, manes streaming back.

And then it came. A shout of anger, a shrill cry of alarm. One voice at first, and then many. And on the beach below, two men started up the cliff. I ran. I raced across that narrow ridge, up toward the moor, on toward the ponies. I heard the creak of wagon wheels, the crack of a whip. Horses snorted, and hooves pounded on the road.

The ponies gazed at me. They turned toward me, and on their sides I saw lanterns hung by leather straps, the glass on one tinted green, the door swinging open. And I knew then what I'd seen from the ship, the beacons that had led us to the Tombstones. They were the lights of wreckers, borne by ponies across the hilltops. These men had carefully, willfully, led our ship to its doom.

And then from the ground behind the ponies, from a hollow in the hills, the wagon came sailing up from the moor in a cloud of frothing dust.

The driver sat hunched forward, his arms lashing with the reins. He looked like a bird, like a raven. The wagon careened around a bend and came straight toward me. The horses were black as tar, glistening with sweat. I could hear their breaths, the thunder of their hooves now on the roadbed, now on the grass.

Ahead was the moor, vast and empty. On each side and behind, the sea stretched from headland to headland, from sky to sky, flecked with the whitecaps of great rolling waves. I had nowhere to go.

The wagon came rushing on. And the men burst from the clifftop behind me, staggering up the slope with their hands pumping at their knees.

I swung to my left and threw myself over the brink.

For an instant there was no sound at all. I seemed to float in that one long second, above the little harbor and village. Then I hit the slope with a thud, rolled and skidded, tumbled and caught myself, tumbled again.

I didn't look back, I didn't look down. I only let myself fall, grabbing when I could at bushes and rock, taking each shock with my knees and my arms, hurtling down in an avalanche of pebbles and dirt. And I spilled out at the bottom, arms wheeling as I stumbled backward across the beach, stumbled and twirled and, finally, fell spread-eagled in the shallows.

I felt I could lie there a long time, with the gulls circling high above, the clouds like a fleet of sailing ships as the sun at last burned through. Across the harbor, sunlight shone on whitewashed walls, on window glass and weathercocks. Beyond the row of seaside buildings, above the homes, the bell tower of the great stone church beckoned. I climbed to my feet and headed toward it.

Suddenly the water beside me erupted in a geyser of

white froth. I heard a clap, felt the ground thud. On the other side, the water burst into a towering column, and then again behind me.

"Get 'im!" The voice came from above me. I had to shield my eyes from the sun to see the men there, gaunt silhouettes. One of them moved, and an instant later the water exploded again, so close that drops splashed on my face. The men were hurling rocks the size of cannonballs.

I ran along the waterline, weaving and ducking. The rocks came faster, splashing in the water to my left, crashing into the shale and sand to my right.

And straight ahead, a plume of dust swirled across the valley. The wagon was racing for the bridge.

I crossed the river, weaving round boats, sprinting for the seawall. I could hear the wagon wheels chattering on the bridge, the shouts of the driver urging on his horses. I reached the wall, only to find the stones slick with weeds. Behind me, the men had started down the cliff.

Along the wall I ran. Gasping. Legs aching. A boat lay prow to the wall, and I stumbled across it. And just beyond there, I found steps. Up I went to a long and empty street paved with cobblestones. On both sides, the buildings rose in overhanging tiers, closing in toward the top.

Somewhere ahead, horses' hooves rang on the paving stones.

I hurried to my left, toward a lane that seemed to lead upward to the church. At the corner was an inn, the Jack-a-Dandy, with a sign of a clown hung from a beam. Across from it hunched a crumbled old blockhouse with a low, open doorway.

The sound of hooves grew louder. It echoed from wall to wall down the canyons of empty streets. It shook the windows and rang in the chains of the Jack-a-Dandy's sign. A drumming, thundering beat, it came from every direction, building and growing like a rising wind. I had little choice; I ducked through the door of the blockhouse, into a darkness cold and dank. There was only one window, a bare slit in the stone, and it let in just a blade of light. But I crept as far from the door as I could, and the hoofbeats boomed in the building.

Through the door I saw a horse hurtle past, saw it from the withers down, dark hair gleaming, a man's boots kicking at the flanks. Another passed in a blur of hooves, a third behind it. Then their clatter faded.

In the silence that followed, I heard a soft and secret sound. A man breathing. And from the shadows and the gloom, a voice rasped in my ear.

"One noise and you're done for," said this voice like a rusted hinge.

Chapter 3
THE LEGLESS MAN

*I*t was too dark to see anything clearly. There was only a shape that seemed to glide instead of walk, that slid across the floor with a squeaky noise. The man circled round, and I squinted at the shadows he made.

"Are you scared?" he asked.

"No," said I, though my voice quavered like a bird's.

"I would be, if I was you," he said. "I'd be sick with affrightment, if you was I."

He moved a little further round the building. He was following the wall, stealthily, toward the door. A shaft of light came through there and lay upon the stones like a shining sword. "You've come from that wreck, ain't you?"

"Yes," I said.

"What was she called?"

"The *Isle of Skye*."

"Yes," he said. "The *Isle of Skye*." Again he moved. Again I heard the little sound, a chuckling like cart wheels.

I closed my eyes. And when I opened them, I could see gray mortar around the stones, wooden beams above. The man kept moving. I could make no sense of his shape; but he was neither standing nor crawling. "How many got off?" he asked.

"I don't know," said I.

His arms swung forward, and he slid—there was no other word for it—into the shaft of light from the doorway. And I understood then: He had no legs. They were both gone, cut off just below the hip. The stumps were clothed in thick woolen pants folded underneath him, and he sat on a wooden trolley that he pushed along with his hands. The hem of his coat was ragged where it scraped the ground.

I'd seen others like him, in London. In this last year of the century, 1799, after years of war against the French, the docks were haunted by sailors maimed or crippled in hideous ways. But none had filled me with the dread I felt as this man came lurching and skidding toward me.

His shoulders were huge, his arms massive. I felt he could crush me in his hands if he liked; he could snap my bones like sticks. But of his face, I could see nothing.

"What's your name?" he asked.

I told him. "John Spencer."

"From where?"

He came closer; I pressed against the wall.

"Where?" he roared.

"London," I said.

I didn't see him move. In an instant he had me by the wrists, both of them in one of his hands. He groped across my chest, and his fingers slithered in and out of my pockets. Then he put his face close to mine, and shapes formed in those awful shadows: the bridge of a thick, twisted nose; tallow-colored cheeks. His huge hand shook me like a rattle.

"Do they know?" he said. "Do they know you're in the village?"

I nodded. "They saw me."

"Then you're done for," said he. "They'll hunt you like a dog." There was a strangeness in his eyes. One looked toward me and one away, and they shone in the shadows like tiny stars. "They'll not stop till they kill you. Mark my words, boy. For it's kill you or hang, it is. Aye, and when they do, you'll be joining your shipmates in the bog upon the moor. And there you'll lie with your lungs full o' muck until the Lord pipes you aloft."

He turned his head and listened. There was a faint beating of hooves, steady as distant rain.

"They're up on the high road," said the legless man. He put one hand on the stone floor and rolled back on his cart. Light spilled in around him, brightening the dark gloom of the blockhouse. I could see, against the wall, a pile of moldy straw and a threadbare blanket, a few narrow shelves propped on sea-worn stones. They held a candle stub and a sad collection of baubles: a bottle cracked at the neck, a whale bone and a seashell, a cutlass handle with holes where the jewels had been picked away—the sort of things a child might collect.

In the moment that had passed, the sound of the horses had doubled in volume.

"They're coming," he said, and yanked on my wrists. I fell toward him onto my knees. He shuffled back on his cart and pulled me after him. "Come," he said.

I could hear each stamp of the hooves, a creaking of leather. "Where?" I asked.

"Damn you, boy." He yanked again.

The legless man was as strong as he looked. He hauled me through the door and, with one more pull, sent me sprawling headlong on the cobblestones. And in those worn and fitted rocks, where they pressed on my cheek and my chest, I could *feel* the horses. The beat of them shook the very stones.

"Up!" he said, and wrenched my wrists.

"Hide me," I cried.

"Not on your life." He let go of my wrists. And I saw, for the first time, that the backs of his hands, his knuckles, were wrapped in bands of tattered leather. On his left hand, on his little finger, was a golden ring that I knew at once.

"That's my father's!" I said.

There was an eagle on it, wings spread. As a child, I'd liked to touch it, to turn it so the light danced upon the gold and the wings seemed to stir and flap. On my father, it was a loose fit on his ring finger; on the legless man, it barely passed the first joint.

"Your father, you say?" His torn lips spread apart, showing broken teeth as brown as sod. "He's wealthy, ain't he? Rich as kings."

"Where is he?" I said.

"This changes things, don't it?" The legless man jerked me close against him. In the daylight he was a horrid figure, a thing all bloated and broken, stuffed into his gray and grimy rags. "You'll have to hide yourself," he snarled. "Or you'll be the death of us all."

The beat of hooves thundered through the lane. The legless man pushed me away. "Now, off with you!" he said, and spun his cart toward the village.

"Help me," I cried again.

"And have them find me with you?" He lurched toward me, his poor stumps of legs spread apart for balance, his fists pumping on the stone. "For seven years I've lived like a dog, hand to mouth in this squalid hole of a house. They call me Stumps, old Stumps the beggar man. And now I'm *that* close"—he rapped his fist on his cart—"to having more gold than I've ever dreamed of. A passage up the coast, one night at sea, and—" He stopped, wheezing. "And you think I'd trade that for you?"

A horse came hurtling down the lane, the rider lashing it on with a short-handled crop. Behind it came another, leaning in the curve, eyes wild and nostrils flared. The legless man made a deep, awful groan. He twirled round. But a third horse appeared behind us, flying at a gallop up the street. And on its back, like a devil, rode the man named Caleb.

The legless man grabbed my arm. He hauled me down until I knelt beside him. And with a twist of his hand, he brought my face up to his.

"Remember this," he said, in a voice I could hardly hear

above the sounds of the horses. "If you put the wreckmen on me, your father will rot where he lies. Only I know where he is, and there he'll stay." His fingers were clamps. My father's ring pressed like a branding iron through my sleeve. "You tell them he's dead, you hear? You tell them he's drowned. Or dead he'll be; mark my words. Dead he'll be, all right. He'll die of thirst, boy. His lips will turn black and rotten. They'll ooze like splattered worms. His tongue will swell and crack, and he'll choke on it—choke on his very own tongue."

He held me there as the horsemen closed round us. They sat in a half circle, leaning forward in their saddles, and the horses heaved wisps of breath through their nostrils. Somewhere in the village another horse was coming, hooves clopping on stone.

With a creak of leather, Caleb swung down from a huge gray mount. His coat rippled around him. His hair, black as tarred rope, swept to his shoulders.

"Well, there's a sight," he said. "The lad crowds on sail like a frigate. But it's Stumps—old dismasted Stumps— what gets the wind of him." He stepped forward. "Give the boy to me."

Stumps made no move to protect me. He passed me over with a nod and a little smile. "Came right to me, Caleb. Just begging for help, he was. Crying out"—this he said in a shrill little voice—" 'Oh! They killed them all. They killed every one but me!' " Then Stumps reached over and gave me a cuff on the back of the head. "So there he is, Mr. Caleb Stratton. And he's the last of 'em, no doubt of that."

There was a look in Stumps's eyes—deep and smoldering—that kept me quiet. A stranger man I'd never met, nor one so horrid. But it wouldn't save my father—or me—to speak of him now. If the wreckers meant to kill me, I could only hope that Stumps would tell Father, when all was done, that I'd gone bravely, with no pleading or tears.

Caleb Stratton took me by the shoulder. The fourth horseman came riding onto the harborfront, his black pacer high-stepping on the cobbles. But no one turned to look; they were all intent on me. And the village seemed as quiet as a graveyard.

The two silent riders stared at me, one with an evil glee that set shivers down my spine, the other with a nervous, frightened glimmer. The nervous one's face was riddled with smallpox. It was that man who spoke, and at that it was little more than a whisper.

"He's only a boy," he said. "Just a boy, Caleb."

"And so was Tommy Colwyn, wasn't he?" Caleb, with my coat bunched in his hand, lifted me nearly clear from the ground. "Have you been up on the moor, Spots?"

Spots shook his head.

"Go, then. Go have a gam with young Tommy Colwyn. Follow the crows, old son; you'll see them from a mile away. His eyes, they're dangling down like watch fobs."

Spots swallowed. "But who's to know?" he said, and licked his lips. "We could turn the boy loose. Let him—"

"You know the law, Spots." Caleb turned to the other man. "Give us your knife there, Jeremy Haines."

The grinning man reached for his belt. A knife appeared in his hand, a long blade that he flipped in his palm, and flipped again to hold it out handle first. He was tall, his stirrups hanging nearly to the horse's knees, and he had to lean far down from the saddle.

Spots looked as though he might be sick. "Least make it quick," he said. "Don't cause the boy no pain."

Caleb took the knife. The way he looked at me, his thumb flicking on the blade, it made me think of Father eyeing the Christmas goose. And it was too much to bear. All my courage and resolve drained away, and I fell to my knees on the cobblestones.

"Bear up," said Stumps, beside me. He sat on his cart like a boy in a wagon, watching with bored interest as these men planned my death so coldly.

"Give him a moment," said Spots. "Let him make his peace, Caleb."

In the stillness, head bowed, I heard the pulse of far-away surf. A gull cried as it wheeled through the sky. The clop of hooves on the stones—the rider came so slowly—was like the chiming of bells. I couldn't see clearly. My eyes, I'm ashamed to say, were wet with tears. I only waited for the knife to strike, and gritted my teeth to stop from screaming.

And then a voice cried out, loud with anger, and the tall man, Haines, said, "Do it, Caleb. That's Simon Mawgan coming."

Caleb grasped my collar. The hooves came faster, harder. I tried to pull free but only twisted onto my back. And there I lay like a dog, flat upon the stones with my neck bared, my head turned away. Caleb crouched beside me.

With a snorting of breath, the black horse barreled into the group of wreckers. It reared up, hooves flailing, and skittered in a tight circle. "Stand back from there," yelled the rider, Simon Mawgan.

Caleb kept his hold on me. "Leave us be," he said.

Mawgan pushed through on his horse until the hooves stamped on the stones beside me. Only dimly could I see him, a man as wide as a barrel, draped in a riding cloak of black and gold. He said, "Let that lad up."

"This is no concern of yours," said Caleb.

"It is if he's from the wreck. Now stand back, I say."

"You don't order me about, Simon Mawgan," said Caleb. But with a last twist of my coat, he let go nonetheless, and stood, the knife balanced in his hands.

"Put that down," said Mawgan. He looked round the group of men. They turned their heads, or lowered them, avoiding his stare like schoolboys caught in a prank. Only Caleb glared back, his eyes like gun slits. "There's been killing enough."

"Not yet there hasn't," said Caleb. "The wreck's not dead."

"The wreck is *mine!*" roared Mawgan. "Or do you argue with that now? Any of you?"

Again the wreckers—all but Caleb—hung their heads. Even the horses seemed to sag and skulk away.

Mawgan laughed. He was rather fat below his cloak, and his cheeks—reddened by wind and sun—shook like jellyfish. " 'Course you don't. I'm surprised at you, Spots. I'd think you a better man than this."

"You're whistling down the wind," growled Caleb. "If

27

that boy lives, we're all off to the knacker's yard. Mark my words, Simon Mawgan. And you'll be with us. Aye, you'll be there."

"We'll see about that," said Mawgan. "Now, help the lad up."

Caleb didn't move. It was Mawgan himself who heaved his bulk from the saddle and held a hand down toward me. "Can you stand?" he said. " 'Course you can. A few scratches and such, but you're fit as a fiddle. Climb on, lad, and I'll ride you up to the moor."

The moor was the last place I wanted to go. But Mawgan, seeing my shock, laughed harder than ever. "I'm taking you home," he said. "I'm taking you up to Galilee."

He made a cup of his hands and gave me a boost. And I settled on the flanks of his big black mount, looking down at Caleb, and at Stumps beside him like a blot of a man. With a sly gesture, Stumps touched my father's ring to his lips.

Mawgan put a foot in the stirrup. Caleb, behind him, raised his knife and slowly pointed the tip directly toward me. He held it there, then just as slowly touched the blade to his neck. The message was clear, delivered in utter silence as the breeze fluttered in the cape of his coat. And I could hear the words in my mind as though he'd spoken them aloud:

"I'm not done with you yet."

Chapter 4
GALILEE

We rode down the waterfront and up through the village, and the horse pranced like a colt, though it carried better than twenty stone upon its back. Simon Mawgan was so roundly fat that I had to spread my arms far apart to keep a hold on his hips. He wore no hat, and his hair was as silver as mist.

He asked my name, and where I came from. And when I told him, he grunted. "You don't look like a Londoner," he said. "You're not so pale and pasty-faced as that."

We talked of the city as we rode through a maze of narrow streets. From cobblestones to dirt; along a twisting lane; through a gateway and up a path barely wider than our knees. Higher we rose, and the buildings spread below us, roof after roof in a solid, jagged field.

"I've been to London," said Simon Mawgan. He turned his head enough to show me his profile. "I like it better here. Room for a horse to run."

The village seemed deserted. Not even a puff of smoke rose from the chimneys. The road turned and climbed again more steeply. And at the top of the hill was the church I'd seen from the far shore, a huge gray building of buttressed walls and a bell tower three stories high. In the arched windows of leaded glass, the faces of saints gazed down at me, their hands clasped and their heads in halos.

We followed a wall past a little graveyard with headstones in staggered rows. Then I saw a movement by the church, and a man stepped out from a side door. He wore black robes that covered him from the neck down, a collar, and spectacles; his head was small and white, like a skull. He stopped in the sunshine—he was smiling—and put on a black hat with an enormous round brim.

"That's the parson," said Mawgan. "Takes his afternoon walk every day in the churchyard." He reined in the horse and adjusted his bulk in the saddle. "Good day to you, Parson Tweed."

The parson waved back, then moved—so gracefully that he might have been a lady—down between the headstones, right up to the wall beside us. He rested his hands on top of the stone.

"Is this the boy I've heard about?" he asked.

"It is," said Mawgan. "I'm taking him to Galilee."

The parson nodded. His gaze flicked over me and away again. "Keep him close to you, Simon. It is providential that you found him before the others could."

"The others *did*," said Mawgan. "Stratton had a knife at his throat."

"Oh, my!" said Parson Tweed. He looked right at me, his eyes dark under the huge brim of his hat.

Mawgan twisted in the saddle. "Stratton is the worst of them all," he told me. "He binds the rest of them together the way a barrel hoop holds the staves. Without him, they would fall apart."

Parson Tweed had a kindly face, but the shadows made it gaunt and sinister. He leaned forward over the wall. "And when those staves come away, what's in the barrel? Hmmm? What's in the barrel then?"

He stared at me, and the wind set little waves rolling across his hat brim. There seemed to be some sly double meaning in his words, but I could make no sense of it.

Then he winked. "We shall see that soon enough." Suddenly he straightened. "Take care of him, Simon."

"I will," said Mawgan. He flicked the reins, and the horse stepped sideways and forward. The parson watched us go.

Mawgan steered the horse onto a dirt lane. "We'll take the sea road," he said. "It's a bit longer, but you'll like it."

At a canter, we circled round the back of the village, then over the stone bridge. In a moment we were up on the moor, and the sea breeze tasted of salt. We didn't pass so close to the cliffs that I could see the Tombstones or the wreck of the *Isle of Skye*. But soon we were right at the Channel, and the road twisted from headland to headland. For a mile or more we rode like that, plumes of dust rising from the hooves. And at each bend, as the cliffs dropped to a patch of sand and rows of wild, wind-driven breakers, Mawgan spoke a few words over his shoulder.

"That's Tobacco Cove below," he said at one. "The *Gehenna* wrecked here in seventy-nine, inbound from the Indies.

"We call this Sheep Cove," he said at the next. "Here the *Northern*, inbound from the Hebrides, came ashore three years ago this month."

Every tiny cove had a name, each for the cargo of a doomed ship. In the mile of shore, Mawgan named sixteen wrecks.

"It's a haunted coast," he said. "Most men won't ride here at night."

Sunset wasn't far off. But at a place he called Sugar Bay, Mawgan stopped to water the horse. He let it drink from a little freshet that dribbled down from the moor to flow thin and sparkling, like a slug's trail, over the stones. I slid down the animal's rump and scooped handfuls of water from the crevices in the rock.

"So," said Mawgan, watching from the saddle, "you're a sailor, are you?"

"Not really," said I. "This was my first voyage."

He smiled faintly. "Where did you go?"

"Greece," I said, "Italy, and Spain."

"Nowhere else?"

I splashed water on my face and then looked up at him through a rainbow. It seemed he was glowering, but when I wiped my eyes I saw only a smile on his face.

"Tell me," he said. He shifted in the saddle. "Where did you load those barrels of wine?"

"Spain," I said.

"What port?"

"I don't know."

"Come on, lad!" He laughed, flinging out his arms. Yet he sounded impatient—nearly angry. "You must know where you were!"

But I didn't. It had been dark when we got there, and we were gone before dawn. I remembered how the barrels had rumbled and thumped, how the ship had sat still in the water like a frightened bird. *"Loading cargo in the dead of night,"* Captain Stafford had said. *"Skulking like thieves."* And I wondered at how odd it was that out of the whole voyage, it was this particular night that caught the interest of Simon Mawgan.

He came down beside me. We sat together above the surf and spray, at the brink of the cliff, and let the horse graze among tufts of grass at the edge of the freshet. Mawgan yawned. "This ship of yours," he said. "The *Isle of Skye.* Who owns her?"

I felt a shiver. What was he driving at? I said, "She was my father's ship."

"Your father's? I see." He moved close beside me. "And where were you going with those barrels of wine?"

"London." I picked up a handful of pebbles and tossed them one by one over the cliff. They fell forever, straight down to the angry sea. I threw six of them before Mawgan spoke again.

"You would go in on the night tide? Is that it? He would be there at the wharf?"

"No," said I.

"What then?"

I tossed another pebble. "He was aboard."

And then Mawgan put his hand on my back, between the shoulders, as though he meant to push me over the edge. He said, "I suppose he drowned in the wreck."

I didn't answer. I drew in a breath and shook all over. Mawgan's hand pressed harder on my back, then suddenly fell away. He must have thought I was crying.

"I'm sorry," he said. "Well, I won't ask you now. But later you'll tell me. You'll tell me the truth of all this."

I didn't know what he meant. Did he know that my father was alive, or was he talking again about the barrels of wine? Whatever it was, I was happy to wait. He stepped into the saddle, and I cast the rest of the pebbles over the cliff, then climbed up behind him.

The day was already late. Our shadows fell far to the east, racing ahead of us along the road, then swinging to our side when Mawgan turned the horse onto a cart path over the moor.

It was a great, empty land that we crossed, but the path snaked in every direction, doubling back and turning again. To the west, the sky had become an ugly blue. And the shadows had darkened until it seemed that beyond each rise lay a vast, gloomy lake that engulfed us as we thundered down. I watched for the crows; I watched for Tommy Colwyn to come rising from the bogs with his eyes dangling at his cheeks. And I thought of my father, hidden away in a place known only to Stumps.

Then, suddenly, Mawgan reined in the horse. "There's

Galilee," he said in a solemn, quiet voice. "I always stop here for a moment. Prettiest sight this side of Plymouth."

"Where?" I said.

"Why, right ahead." He raised a hand and pointed.

I had to lean over to see around him. And there, under his arm, windows aglow with lamplight, was a white house twice the size of my London home. Behind it was a cottage and a small stable. Surrounded by hedgerows, nestled in a valley by a brook, the house was so sheltered from the breeze that the chimney smoke lay around it like a wreath.

Mawgan set the horse forward at a walk. The saddle creaked as he turned slightly toward me. "I like it on the moor," he said. "I'm far enough from the sea that I only rarely hear the surf. Yet I'm close enough I can hear a pistol shot."

It was a curious way to gauge distance. Before I could answer, he was talking again.

"Mary will have the dinner ready. Oh, she's a fine cook." We passed through the hedgerows. There was no gate; the road merely ended there at the house. "With any luck she'll have starry-gazy."

I said, "What's starry-gazy?"

"Why, pilchards, lad. Pilchard pie." Simon Mawgan shook his head. "You say you're from London, and you don't know starry-gazy?"

He swung his leg across the horse's neck and slipped from the saddle as easily as a boy. I sprang down beside him.

"Eli!" he cried. Then, "Blast him! Where are you, Eli?"

Out from the cottage came a teetering, shuffling figure. He was like a bit of old sausage—thin and brown and bent—and he came with his arms cocked back, as though someone behind was pushing him on. He saw me but asked no questions. Without a word at all, he took the reins and led the horse toward the stables.

Mawgan clapped a hand on my shoulder. "Eli's a fright to look at, but he gets the work done. Don't try talking to him." He ushered me toward the house. "He's got no tongue, you see."

"No tongue?" I said.

"A dreadful thing," said Mawgan. "A wicked thing."

The smoke smelled of peat and lay on the ground as thick as sea mist. It swirled round our legs as we climbed to the porch, then flurried with us in through the door. And there I stopped.

I'd been to the homes of barons and lords. I'd been to palaces and castles. But none was as fine or as rich as the home of Simon Mawgan. The entire floor of the parlor was covered by a huge Persian carpet, and half of that was covered again by another carpet twice as thick. In the middle stood a round table made from a ship's wheel. Pulled up to its rim were high-backed chairs plush with leather, and on its polished top sat chalices of silver, crystal decanters, rows and rows of delicate glasses. Ships' figureheads were mounted like hunting trophies; a round-topped sea chest stood below a corner window. All around, on every shelf and level surface, were golden figurines, intricate carvings of wood, and small boxes inlaid with shells and sparkling jewels. And this was only one room of the house.

Through a doorway I could see a dining table so big that it was laid like a trestle across the barrels of English cannons.

Mawgan popped his thumbs into his waistband. "Everything here," he said, "comes from the sea."

"From wrecks," I said.

He squeezed my shoulder and smiled. "That's right, my boy. It's a bountiful thing, the sea."

This made me more angry than I could say. For every bauble that he owned there was a drowned sailor. For each bit of finery a man lay buried in the moor. I shook off his hand and turned away.

"What's the matter?" he said. "Why, John Spencer, I do believe you're angry."

I didn't look at him. I stood there, shaking.

"Oh," he said then. "Oh, I see. Why, you've come from the other side, haven't you?" He touched me again, his fingers on my back. "Well, I'll ask you this: Did *I* steer those ships onto the rocks? Did *I* miss stays or lose my way on a dark night? 'Course I didn't. So why—"

"You wrecked the *Isle of Skye*," I told him. I straightened and looked him right in the eye. "You used false lights to lure us—"

"Who told you that?" said Mawgan. He fixed me with a hawk's glare. "Who told you there were false lights?"

"I saw them," said I.

"Then you saw wrong."

"I did not," I said. "They used lights to lead us ashore, and then they killed us. Caleb and the others. They murdered everyone."

"Do you *know* that?" said Mawgan. His fingers no longer merely touched me; they gripped like talons. "Do you know for a fact that they killed everyone but you?"

His face, so jovial before, had become fierce as a lion's. White spittle bubbled at the corners of his mouth. He shook me. "Do you?"

There was a sound behind him, like a clap, and a girl's voice spoke sharply. "Uncle Simon! You're scaring him."

His face changed on the instant, the anger in it melting again to kindness. By the time he turned away from me, Simon Mawgan was smiling like an angel. "Mary," he said.

She was beautiful. Strong and tanned, she stood in the doorway with her arms crossed. She was my age or maybe younger by a year, and her hair—with the lamplight shining in it—looked the way the sea does on a rosy dawn. "Who is this?" she asked.

Mawgan laughed. "This is John Spencer," he said. "A shipwrecked sailor."

"You were shouting at him."

"I'm sorry," he said. "But I hear stories like those, and they make me angry. I like a good wreck as much as the next man, but I won't abide false lights and I won't stand for murder."

"I know," said Mary. "But Uncle, you weren't there last night."

"No matter," said Mawgan. "I know the men of Pendennis."

Mary nodded. "I'll put the dinner up," she said, and slipped away like a butterfly.

Mawgan took off his coat and hung it on a peg. He reached out for mine, then glanced toward the door. His voice dropped to a whisper. "I'll tell you this," he said. "If any man lives from that wreck, his life isn't worth tuppence. Not tuppence, you hear?"

I gave him my coat. It was wet and dirty, heavy with salt.

"We might all be in peril if one got ashore," he said. He bent over toward me. "So tell me. Is there anyone else?"

I was afraid to lie. He would see it in my eyes as plain as a signal. But a vision of Stumps rose in my mind, his face bloated like sewer gas. *Your father will rot where he lies.* I had no idea whom I could trust, and so I decided to trust no one at all.

"Well?" said Mawgan. His brow narrowed. "Did someone else get ashore?"

"No one I saw," I told him.

He stared at me for a moment. Then: "Very well," he said. "Now come and eat."

We sat down to a dinner that would have fed a whole watch of seamen. There were pasties and lammy pies, a huge slab of pork, a tower of bread. "That's wheat bread," said Mawgan, his mouth overflowing. "You won't see cornmeal or barley bread in this house." Mary laid it down, went back for more, fetched plate after plate as Mawgan shoveled it down.

Finally, Mary came from the kitchen with a thing so awful I could hardly bear to look. It was a pie, with a crust as smooth and brown as a sandy beach. But through it poked the heads of fish, thrusting up as though she'd baked them alive as they floundered for air. Their big cooked eyes bulged toward the ceiling.

"Ah," said Mawgan. "The starry-gazy." He cleared a vast spot, pushing with his elbows at dishes and bowls.

Mary laughed. She put the plate at the edge of the table and went past us to the door. "That edn't for you." Her Cornish accent sounded like music. "I made that'm for Eli."

"For Eli?"

"Now, don't go on, Uncle. You've got plenty as it is." She took a shawl from its hook and tied it round her chin. "Starry-gazy's all the poor old soul can eat."

Mawgan snorted. "Last week lammy pies was all the wretch could eat." But he let her take the plate and step out through the door with no more fight than that. He launched a ferocious attack on the pasties that lasted until Mary was back. "Coffee," he said as she took off her shawl.

"It will have to be tea." She was smiling, brightened by her walk. "We haven't had a coffee wreck in the longest time."

I was stung by the way that even Mary could talk, with such nonchalance, of what came from the drowning of sailors. I told them I was overcome by the rich food, by the warmth of the house. And I let Mawgan lead me to an upstairs room, where I fell asleep to the sound of laughter below.

Chapter 5
A ROW OF BODIES

My father came to me again in my dreams. He stood at the stern of our little brig, his hands clasped behind his back, his beard parted by the wind. He was giving orders in a calm voice, and it was I who obeyed every one.

First I was at the helm, then up in the topmast, then down in the waist hauling all by myself on a halyard. And wherever I went, Father followed. Each time he came he was thinner and weaker. His lips turned black, his eyes grew big as eggs. He begged me for water, and he asked for his ring. "Have you seen it, John? Have you seen my ring?"

Then he sent me below, down to the bilge. And he came crawling behind me on hands and knees, crawling from the darkness with rats all round him. His eyes had popped from his head, and they dangled on bloody strings, swaying against his cheeks. He was begging, but I couldn't understand him. And when he opened his mouth it was full of blood, and I saw that his tongue was torn away.

I woke screaming. I didn't know where I was. And then I felt a hand on my forehead, and it was Mary leaning over me.

"Hush," she said. "Hush, John." She touched my lips, my eyelids. "You were dreamin', is all."

She scooped up a bundle of clothes from a chair, then went to the window and opened the curtains. It was morning, though the sky was darkly red.

"You'll want to be getting up," she said. "Breakfast is waiting. Then you can come with me across the moor."

"And your uncle?"

"He's off on his business." She did an imitation of him, her cheeks puffed out: " 'Can you keep an eye on him, Mary? 'Course you can.' " She laughed gaily. "He took a fancy to you, I think. You must remind him much of Peter."

"Who's Peter?" I asked.

"He wouldn't have told you. Peter was his son." She dropped her bundle on the bed. "He found these for you. Pair of breeches and a jersey."

There was a coat too, and a neckerchief. They looked nearly new. "Were they Peter's?" I asked.

"No," she said. "But Uncle told me that the boy who had them last was no bigger than you."

Mary turned her back as I dressed. I said, "What happened to Peter?"

"He was drownded."

42

The clothes fit well enough, but there was a rip in the jersey, by the shoulder. It looked about the size of a cutlass blade.

"I can mend that'm for you," said Mary when she saw me with my fingers poking through the hole. And after breakfast, as I sat on the sea chest by the window, she leaned over me with a strand of yarn between her lips, and she pulled and poked at the cloth.

"Mary?" I said. "Was Peter drowned at a wreck?"

The needle stopped for only a moment. "Yes," she said.

"He was a wrecker?"

"No." She tossed back her hair. "He was very young, John. But don't ask about that. It's a thing Uncle doesn't like to have talked about."

She went back to her work, and I watched the needle pass in and out of the cloth. Her fingers were strong, more like a man's than a girl's.

Then I said, "Who was Tommy Colwyn?"

The needle stabbed against my skin. "Sorry," said Mary. "Who was he?"

She tied a knot, then broke the yarn with a quick tug. "How do you know about Tommy?"

"The men in the village," I said. "They talked of him."

"And what did they say?"

"That he's found on the moor under a cloud of crows. That his eyes hang out like watch fobs."

Mary drew in a breath. She turned away from me, her face to the window.

"Was *he* a wrecker?" I asked, and she nodded. "He was caught, was he?"

"And hanged in chains."

I shuddered. That was an awful thing to see, a man hanged in chains. I'd seen the pirates at Execution Dock, their dead bodies left to blacken and rot, picked at by birds, swinging in the wind for weeks or even months as a lesson to others.

"And he hangs there still?" I asked.

Mary nodded. "But Tommy wasn't hanged for the wrecking," she told me. "They found him on the moor, with a spade in his hands and a row of bodies not quite buried."

There was a catch in her breath as she said it. Her shoulders drooped. "It was the wreckers they wanted. They said to Tommy, 'Give us their names and you'll go free.' He weren't there at the wrecking, but he knew who was. He said, 'I won't tell you that.' So they hanged him. Only a boy, and they hanged him."

"He deserved it," I said.

"No." She touched the window. "You don't understand, John. You don't know how it is."

"Tell me, then."

"Not in the morning. I don't think about this in the mornings." Her cheeks were red as rose hips. She took my hand and pulled me up. "Let's go now."

"Where?"

"Across the moor."

There were ponies in the stable, and we rode them bareback, laughing as we raced over the empty land. Mary was a better rider than me, sitting with her skirts hiked up and flowing in the wind. We splashed through brooks, hurdled crumbling walls, ran and ran with the sun at our backs.

"This way!" cried Mary, and veered to the south, to the top of a knoll.

She beat me by a furlong and was already seated on the ground—flush-faced, her skirts smoothed around her—when I gained the summit and slid from the pony.

"Edn't it beautiful?" said Mary.

It was. I felt I could see halfway to London from the top of that rise. To the south was the Channel, with a glower of clouds over faraway France: a gale in the offing. Westward, the rooftops of Pendennis were nestled in their cove, the church standing above them like a block of gray stone. But it was to the east that I looked.

And Mary guessed what I was thinking. "Uncle will put you on the next packet," she said. "You'll be home in a fortnight. Maybe less."

"But home to what?" I said.

"Why, your mother. Your father. They'll be worried to the death about you."

"I have no mother," I told her. "She died when I was very young."

"And your father?" Mary was looking up at me, surrounded by her skirts like a flower.

"He was on the *Isle of Skye*."

"Oh, dear," she said. "I'm sorry."

I wanted to tell her the truth. I felt I *had* to tell someone. In two weeks, maybe less, I'd be sailing off to leave my father at the mercy of the legless man. And to have him think forever that I had died in the wreck.

45

"Have you no uncles?" asked Mary. "No aunties?"

"No." I sat beside her. The ponies stood off at a distance, watching us with round, wondering eyes.

"So you have no one," she said. "You poor thing."

Her eyes were so kind, so gentle, that I knew I could trust her. "Mary," I said, barely a whisper. "My father is still alive. He's hidden somewhere in the village."

"How do you know that?"

"Stumps," I said. "He—"

"That horrible man?" She shook her head. "No, John. You can't believe what he tells you."

"But he had my father's ring," I said.

"He collects things, John. Little baubles. He's like a magpie that way; he always has been."

"It's more than that," I said. "I *know* it's true."

I told her how I'd sheltered in the blockhouse and how Stumps had found me in the dark. I told her everything that had happened from then until the moment that she found Simon Mawgan shouting at me in the doorway of the house. She listened in silence, her knees drawn up and her arms around them.

"So I can't tell anyone," I said. "Or Stumps will kill my father. And I don't know what to do."

"Uncle will know," said Mary.

"But he's one of them!" I cried.

Mary laughed. "You don't know my uncle."

"I know he's a wrecker," I said.

"He's not."

"They all are."

"And then so am I?"

"Well, maybe not," I said. "But Tommy Colwyn—"

"Stop it!" Mary leapt to her feet. "It's not the people, John. It's this country. This wasteland."

I shook my head.

"The men of Pendennis were miners once. They went down in the ground for a shilling a day, down so deep that the sea rushed in at their feet. And in the days of rain and floods they couldn't work at all, and they'd go for weeks without earning a farthing. Others went fishing; all day they spent out in the fog and the storms for a bucket of pilchards. That was all a boy could hope to do. He could drown in the mines or drown in the sea."

She wrung her hands, then buried them in the folds of her skirt. "You've seen the land. Most of it won't grow potatoes, and it won't graze sheep. There were people so hungry that they scraped up limpets from the Tombstones. But the Mawgans were wealthy. They had Galilee, and they owned the best of the mines. The Mawgans never suffered like the rest."

She took a breath. Her eyes seemed as round as the ponies'. "Once in a while—in a very great while—a ship would come to ruin on the rocks. And there would be food then, and wine, and huge heaps of things just waiting to be carried off and sold for pounds and pounds. And for once it was the Mawgans who suffered."

"Because no one was left to work the mines?"

"Not only that." Mary bunched her skirt in her fists. "By law the Mawgans had 'right of wreck.' We still do. Any ship that comes ashore in the great arc of St. Elmo's Bay—anywhere between Wrinkle Head and Northground—legally belongs to my uncle. His father had right of wreck; his grandfather did before that. The oldest man in Pendennis can remember a Mawgan standing in the ruins of a tea wreck, swatting at men who came for the chests, yelling that they were his, that it all belonged to him."

Mary turned toward the sea. "Only rarely did ships come ashore on the Tombstones. They might wreck *there*"—she pulled a hand free and pointed to the east—"or there, or there, or there. So the people followed them. Whenever a ship was caught on the lee shore, the whole village—women and children and men—tracked it along the coast. For days they wandered with it, back and forth, back again. And they prayed, John, they knelt and prayed that the poor ship would meet its end before it got to the next village, before it met the crowd that had set out from there with their own axes and picks."

She was staring at the gray waters of the Channel. Her voice dropped, and she shivered. "The law said that anything that came from a wreck was free for salvage. But for it to be a wreck, no one could survive—not man or beast. If one person—if so much as a dog—made it safely ashore, then it weren't really a wreck at all. 'The wreck edn't dead,' is what they'd say. So it was the law, John, that made the devil's work of wrecking."

"Because," I said, "they killed the people who got to shore."

"Yes. It came to that." She sat again, close beside me. "But it got worse. It got much worse."

Chapter 6
THE HAUNTED COVE

Mary sat on the grass, her face to the sea. Her voice grew faint and faraway, as though she talked from a different place and a different time.

"I only once saw them use the false beacons," she said. "It was the night of a terrible storm. You could hardly stand in the wind, it was that strong. And a ship came running down toward the shore."

"When was this?" I asked.

"Seven years ago," said she. "I was only a child." She closed her eyes. "We lay in a row along the cliffs and watched that ship. The waves were breaking right over the decks, and we could hear the sails blowing out — *boom, boom* — one after the other. It was Caleb Stratton who said, 'Show them a light.' I remember him standing when everyone else was flat on the ground, standing in the rain and the wind, with that big black beard of his like a mask on his face. 'We done it before,' he said. 'Show 'em a light and they steer straight for it.' Uncle Simon would have none of it — I remember him shouting — and most of the people felt the same way. But Caleb had a power and a strength, and there were always a few who would follow him. Stumps — he still had his legs then, though not for long — ran off to fetch a lantern. They tied it to the tail of a pony that they walked across the cliffs. I remember the way it flared in the wind, the way the men laughed. Those poor wretched sailors; they must have thought they saw the masthead of a ship going into harbor. And they followed like lambs. Right to the Tombstones."

"Did you see that?" I asked.

"No. They sent us home, the women and children."

"And your uncle?"

"He stayed at the cliffs." Mary lay back and put her hand over her eyes. "The storm blew all night. And Uncle Simon came home in the morning, all bloodied and bruised, soaked with salt water. He had tried to stop them, he said. He had tried to put out the light, and they attacked him."

"He told you this?"

"And I believed him," said Mary. "He poured a huge glass of brandy. It shook in his hands. Then he told me how the ship drove up on the rocks and how the masts fell, sails and all. The men were standing on the clifftop, Caleb and the others, laughing and dancing like boys at a game. And Uncle — this is what he told me — followed them down to the beach and took up an axe. And in the darkness he—" She stopped, breathing softly.

"What?" I asked.

Mary spread her fingers and peered at me between them. "That was the night Stumps lost his legs."

Suddenly the day seemed very cold. I could imagine the scene as Mary described it, Stumps writhing on the ground as the axe rose and fell. But just as easily I could imagine a cable cinching on his legs, Simon Mawgan wielding a lantern instead of an axe.

"A lot of men drownded that night," said Mary. "And since then my uncle's made sure that they never again used the lights."

"But they do," I said.

"Oh, no," she said. "They don't."

"I saw them." I turned to her, almost pleading. "I saw them from the ship."

"It's quite impossible, John. You must have seen stars, or maybe—"

"I saw the ponies on the cliff. They had lanterns on their backs."

"Are you sure?" said Mary. "Maybe they were boxes. Maybe they were—"

"They were lanterns," said I.

"Oh, dear." She closed her eyes. "Uncle Simon will be very angry to hear this."

"Angry?" I laughed. "He did it. He wrecked the *Skye*, and he wrecked others before her."

"No!" said Mary.

"Look at his house. All those things." I thought of my bedroom. On the wall hung a quadrant that a sailor had used to find his way from the stars. In Simon Mawgan's house, it was a rack to hold socks.

"You judge him too harshly," she said. "He's not an evil man; he's really not. He only takes what the law gives him—a payment, or a share, from the wrecks that God brings about."

"God wrecks the ships?" I asked.

"If not Him, then who else?"

"It was men who wrecked the *Isle of Skye*," I told her.

"And it was my uncle who saved you from it," she said. "And edn't that the truth? Edn't it? If he *did* wreck your ship, then why did he help you?"

I had no answer for that. But still I wasn't sure. "Where was he when it happened?"

"With Parson Tweed. He was called away to see the parson." She sat up. "And if that won't convince you, then I suppose nothing will."

At that moment I believed her. How could I not? He was her uncle, and Mary seemed so sure of him, so loving. Of course I believed her.

"Now, come on," said Mary. "We've a fair distance to go yet."

"To where?" I asked.

"Why, to the Tombstones."

We rode south, and met the road at Coffee Cove. But when it turned inland, we kept to the cliffs, and soon came to our destination.

We pressed the ponies right to the brink. It scared them to stand there. They shied away, their eyes rolling as they tossed their heads. Mary kept hers steady while mine pranced sideways and pawed at the ground.

"They never like it here," said Mary. "They smell the fear and the dying."

Below us, the sea looked gray and cold. In endless rows, the waves gathered themselves, towering high, then rushed at the rocks in a heaving crash of surf and spray. The water whirled among those spikes of stone, leaping up in great white spouts, blasting into sheets, flying as spindrift across the cove. There was nothing left of the poor *Isle of Skye*; it was as though the wreck had never happened. But high on the beach, where the waves reached like fingers to the cliffs, were the same heaps of rope and shattered wood. And the gulls still circled round and round.

"They always gather where there's been a wreck," said Mary, seeing the way I stared. "People say when a sailor drowns that his soul becomes a gull."

It was a nice thought. I studied them, the birds turning gray, then silver, as they flashed across the sun. Could one be old Cridge, another Danny Riggins, the foretopman, free now to spin through the sky?

"I hate this cove," said Mary. "It's the worst place of them all." The wind lifted her hair, and above her the gulls cried like babies. "It's haunted, John."

Her uncle had said the same thing, with the same little shiver in his voice.

"You can feel it, can't you? The sadness." With a press

of her heels, Mary let the pony move back from the edge. Mine went with it; I couldn't stop it. "You see corpse lights here," she said.

"Ghosts, you mean?"

"Not as you'd think of them." She looked at me, and her eyes were as gray as the sky. "All you see are lights. Pale blue lights that move along the beach or across the cliffs. At night and in the fog. Slowly, slowly they go: like a funeral march." Suddenly she laughed. "Oh, it makes me scared just to think of it. When people see the corpse lights, they run away."

"Have you seen them?"

She shook her head. "Years ago—before I was born—people heard a ship come ashore. It was a full moon, and flat calm, but in the village they heard a shout—a scream—and then the smashing of a ship. They all came, the whole village, and they stood right here along the cliffs. They stood and listened to the screaming, to the crack of wood and the thunder as the masts came down. But the bay was empty, John; there was no ship."

I looked down at the Tombstones, and I saw that the sea was changing. We watched the wind ripple across the surface, black bands that thickened and thinned as they raced toward us. Behind them, whitecaps bloomed.

"The air was deathly still," said Mary. "The sea was flat as a field, but they could hear the roar of heavy surf. And then, for a moment, they did see a ship. It was a ghost, a pale, shimmering hull, and they could see right through it to the Tombstones and the moonlight on the water. An old man of the village—he's been dead twenty years—said,

'The *Virtue*! She wrecked here eleven year ago.' " And as they watched, the corpse lights came. They rose up from that ship that wasn't there, and came across the water."

Mary shivered. "The people ran away. They all turned and ran, except for one man who stayed behind. He shouted after them; he taunted them. He was going down to the beach, he said. He wasn't scared of a few little lights. But he was never seen again, John. They say the ghost ship carried him off."

"And the lights?" I asked.

"Uncle Simon used to tell me if I stayed out at night, the corpse lights would get me." Mary smiled. "All children are told the same. And a month ago there was a ship embayed. She came in the night, and the men were waiting with lanterns. But they saw the corpse lights right there on the beach."

Mary pointed down the cliff. "It was one light, moving along. Caleb Stratton was there, and Jeremy Haines, Spots, and the others. And they all ran away; Caleb tried to stop them, but he couldn't. In the morning the ship was gone. Some people said it was never there at all. It was the *Virtue* come back, they said, and she was looking for crew. They say the corpse lights are dead men. Dead men alive."

I looked down at the sea, and I thought of old Riggins, who'd told me stories of specters and ghost ships as the *Isle of Skye* sailed on a rolling sea. And I longed for those days, and wished I could live them again. I ached to ride a tall ship through the night, with the sails rising above me like patches over the stars. I had felt I would die if Father doomed me to work in the dusty prison of an office. I remembered him saying—he loved to say it—"You'll never make a seaman." Our voyage had been a lesson, to teach me that he was right. "Too many dangers by half," he had said, hoping to save me from the very thing that had befallen us. I looked down at the sea, and I sighed.

Mary tugged my sleeve. "Come on, John," she said. "I'm tired of the sadness here."

As we backed and turned the ponies, a gust rose up the cliff and tangled their manes.

"I'll show you my garden," said Mary. "My secret garden."

It wasn't far. Nestled between the cliffs and the road, it lay in a little gully hidden by a tangle of bush. There, in a patch of soil about the size of a door, Mary had planted wildflowers.

"I call it my memory garden," she said. "For each wreck, I've started a plant." She turned her head away and crouched suddenly on the ground. "It's silly, really, edn't it?"

"No," I said. "It's not." The flowers grew in rows, twelve abreast, filling the space. A little farther down the gully, she'd cleared the ground for a new plot. The soil was broken but empty, waiting like a fresh grave.

"They grow so well here," said Mary. "It's a funny thing. I never water them, never weed them." She groomed the flowers, arranging them on their stalks. "I can't explain it. But it's sort of like magic, don't you think?"

She wasn't looking at me. She stroked each flower, then touched its leaves, as though these were little people she hovered over.

She lifted her skirts and held them clear of the flowers. "There's so many. So many flowers. And each time I plant one, I cry." She walked on her toes between them, up to the top of the garden. "Sometimes I imagine this whole bluff"—she spread her arms, and her skirts tumbled loose—"all that you see, covered with flowers, each for a wreck."

We made our way back to the ponies. As though by agreement, we didn't ride them, but led them instead up toward the road.

"Sometimes I can't bear it," said Mary. "I can hear it from the house, the screaming."

The wind gusted past us. I heard a distant sound of horses and leather.

"I want to stop it," said Mary.

"You couldn't," I said. "It would be you against all of Pendennis."

She shook her head. "It edn't the whole village, John. It's just a few of the worst. Like Caleb Stratton and Jeremy Haines. Without them, the wrecking would stop. Without them, people would come to save the sailors, and not to kill them."

I said, "Parson Tweed told me Caleb is the leader."

"It looks that way," said Mary. "But I think there's someone else, someone secret. Caleb Stratton edn't very smart. I think he's like a puppet, and this person works him and tells him what to do. I have to find out who he is, the puppet master."

I wondered: Could it be Simon Mawgan, his house packed full of plunder from the wrecks? I was sure it wasn't old Eli, and I knew it wasn't Stumps. But I'd met no one else, apart from the parson and Mary herself.

"Who might it be?" I asked.

"Someone in the village, I'm sure. Someone I know. Whoever it is, he can go anywhere he wants with nobody wondering. And only Caleb Stratton will know his secret."

I sighed. I plucked at the grass.

"But it edn't so bad," said Mary. "I have a plan."

I looked at her, and she glanced back for a moment, her eyes covered by her lashes. "Tell me," I said.

She blushed. "You'll think me foolish."

"I won't," I said.

She didn't talk until we reached the road. And for a moment she stood combing her fingers through the pony's mane.

"The next time a ship wrecks on the Tombstones, I'm going to swim out to it," she said. Her hands ran across the pony's shoulder, down the ridge of its back. "I'll get aboard somehow, and I'll tie myself to the mast. And if they want the wreck, they'll have to . . . to kill me."

"They will," I said.

She nodded. "Maybe. Maybe not."

It wasn't much of a plan. But I could see by her face—the lines that hardened round her eyes—that she meant to try. "I know this, John," she said in her Cornish way. "Whichy way it goes, it's better than doing naught."

She was braver than I. As we stood there at the edge of the moor, the wind combing back the tufts of grass, she waited—I think—for me to agree, to throw my lot in with her wild idea. But nothing in the world would get me back on the Tombstones, back on the deck of a doomed ship to face Caleb Stratton and his men waiting there with axes and pikes.

The ponies whinnied and tugged at their bridles. Mary stood her ground, her arm rising and falling as her pony pulled at her. She never took her eyes from me.

And I heard again the horses and the creaking of wheels. "Someone's coming," I said.

I couldn't tell at first where the sound was coming from. Then, toward the village, I saw a swirl of dust blowing off across the moor. And a moment later two black horses and a clattering wagon came sailing up over the rise.

"It's the Widow," said Mary. "The widdy-woman."

Chapter 7
THE EVIL EYE

With a great clamor of pounding hooves and groaning wood, the wagon swayed toward us in a boil of dust. The horses were bigger than any I'd ever seen, and they snorted in the harness. The driver cried out to them and shook his reins, and the wagon shimmied across the road. He was a small man, hunched in the seat, wearing a bully-cocked hat white with dust, a neckerchief across his nose and mouth. And over his shoulder rose a woman's face and a flowing mass of pure white hair.

"They say the Widow commands the winds," said Mary. "She raises tempests."

The Widow stood up and held on to the driver's shoulders as the wagon lurched between the ruts. Her face was brown as old parchment, wrinkled like a much-folded map. She looked right at me, with eyes that glowed pink as embers of coal. When the wagon was a dozen yards off, she cried out; not to the driver, but to the horses themselves. The animals bared their teeth and tossed their heads, huffing clouds of fog as though it was smoke they breathed. They slowed to a walk, and their hooves beat a steady march on the roadbed.

The Widow kept her hands on the driver, her feet spaced wide apart. She turned only her head, and stared at me as the wagon rolled past. It was a deep, probing look, and her eyes burned with an awful hatred. I stared back, because I couldn't take my eyes away. I could feel her reaching into my mind, as though fingers crawled in my skull. And still her head swung round as the horses marched on, until it seemed she was looking right back between her shoulders. Then she reached a hand toward me and curled her two middle fingers toward her palm. "Get back!" she said. "Get back where you were!" And she stood like that, staring and pointing, until the wagon rose on the next crest, and dropped out of sight. It looked as though she was sinking into the ground.

"She's put the evil eye on you," said Mary. "You'll have to watch for her."

Our poor ponies had gone half mad. They stood trembling, their ears pressed catlike against their skulls, their eyes rolled up to the whites like hard-boiled eggs. "Hush," said Mary to hers. "Hush now." It flinched when she touched it, then calmed slowly under her hand.

"The Widow's tetched," she said, tapping her head. "People say she's a witch, but I think she's just crazy. Years ago she saw her brother drownded. Before that, her husband; his body was never found."

"But the way she looked at me. It was—"

"She thinks you're him come back from the dead." Mary grabbed the pony's mane and sprang up on its back. "It's not just you," she said, looking down. "She thinks the same of any man or boy who gets ashore from a wreck."

"How does she know I came from a wreck?"

"News travels fast." Mary watched as I hauled myself onto the pony. "They probably know of you in Polruan by now, and that's better than twenty mile from here."

We started off down the road, side by side in the Widow's wake. The dust from her wagon flurried ahead of us like a little tornado.

"So there have been others," I said.

"Others what?" asked Mary.

"Saved from a wreck."

"A few," she said, "have reached the shore."

It was all she would say. And then she shouted at me to race her, and set her pony into a gallop for home.

Though we ran at a breakneck speed, we never caught up with the Widow. The cloud of dust moved along at the same pace as ourselves until we turned inland on the path to Galilee. We hurtled round that bend. Mary was a length ahead—the hind hooves of her pony kicked divots of sod as we swung out onto the edge of the moor. She glanced back, and I saw her face through a veil of hair. I leaned forward like a jockey, stretched so flat along the mane that I peered between the pony's ears. I could feel it writhing under me, pounding along like a boat in a seaway. I edged ahead, fell back a bit, surged forward again. Neck and neck we flew over the rise where Simon Mawgan had stopped to look at the view. Mary was laughing. "The loser," she cried, "has to stable the ponies."

Into the glen the ponies ran shoulder to shoulder, paced so closely that their hooves sounded like a single animal. I was on the side closest to the manor; Mary would have to pass ahead or behind.

The path turned to the left. Mary, on the inside, inched ahead. She too was lying flat, her hands right up at the bits. The dust rose around us.

The path straightened, then curved the other way. I could see the opening in the hedgerows. Mary was beside me, her lips dusted gray. And then she was gone.

I could spare only a glance. She'd reined in the pony and passed so close behind that I'd felt a jolt as its head brushed the flanks of mine. And now she was running across the open moor.

As I slowed for the opening, Mary braced her knees on her pony's ribs. She hugged its neck. She aimed it straight for the hedgerow.

I passed through the gateway. And ahead, to the right, Mary's pony came soaring over the hedge. It flew as though winged, carrying her up in an arch, its forelegs clear by a foot, its belly just touching the leaves. And atop it sat Mary, graceful as an angel. She seemed to hang there for a moment, absolutely still. Then she came rushing down, and the pony's hind legs crashed through the hedgerow in a litter of twigs and old leaves. The pony stumbled forward, almost touching its knees to the ground, then straightened and stopped. Mary had beaten me by a dozen yards.

She laughed when I pulled up beside her. "You know where the stable is," she said. "And if you see Uncle Simon, tell him there's a special treat for supper. I made it this morning."

The ponies seemed hardly troubled by their run. They trotted ahead to the stable door, anxious as dogs to be back at their home. And as I came up behind them, I heard Simon Mawgan's voice from inside the building, so loud with anger that he could have been standing beside me.

"Damn your eyes!" he said. "I told you to watch that boy, didn't I? Well, where did they go, then?"

I heard no answer. He might as well have been speaking to himself.

"Just show me!" he shouted.

One of the ponies thumped against the door. Something clattered inside, and Mawgan roared, "Who's there?"

I opened the door. The stable smelled of hay. A dust of corn and oats floated in the light, and through this golden haze I saw Mawgan deep in the shadows with a crop in his raised hand. The other man was lying in a stall; I could see only his boots, and they pushed at the floor as he scrambled back.

The ponies crowded at me, pushing me in.

Mawgan lowered the riding crop and tapped it on his knee. "Where have you been?" he said.

"We went riding," I told him.

"Where?" he barked.

"Across the moor," said I.

"I'll ask once more." He took a step toward me. The

65

ponies clomped through the stable and went each to its stall. "Where have you been?"

"The Tombstones," I said.

"The Tombstones." The crop tap-tapped against his leg. "I didn't say you could go gallivanting across the countryside."

I said, "I didn't know I was a prisoner."

Maybe my boldness surprised him. More likely, he saw through it to the fear inside. He laughed heartily. "A prisoner, you say? No, no, my lad. I was worried about you, is all. I suppose it was Mary's idea, was it? 'Course it was. Headstrong girl, that one."

Then, without turning, he spoke to the man in the stall. "Get up from there. Give the boy a hand with the ponies."

It was Eli, the shriveled old man with no tongue. He came out cautiously, like a weasel from its den. But from the way he held his arms, I could see that the riding crop had done him no harm.

"You've run those ponies hard," said Mawgan. "Put blankets on them, John, then come to the house." He left without another word.

Eli fetched blankets and a comb, all the time watching the door. I held my hand out for a blanket, looking not at him but at the ponies. Mawgan was right; they were starting to tremble with cold sweats. And suddenly Eli clutched my arm.

There were bits of straw stuck in his hair, another piece lying aslant across his shoulder. His face was shrunken and cracked like old mud. And the sounds he made, from deep in his throat, were the croakings of a frog.

I pulled away from him; I couldn't bear his touch. But he came at me again, bent and shuffling, and grabbed my sleeve with a hand that was more like a claw, the skin stretched over talon fingers. He made the sounds again, the awful groans and warbles, and cast another frightened glance at the door.

I dropped to my knees and hauled him down beside me. I swept a bit of dirt clear of old straw and scratched words with my finger: "Show me."

He yanked on my arm, and yanked again, until I looked up at his face. He shook his head so violently that bits of straw flew like arrows from his hair.

"You can't read?" I said. "You can't write?"

Again he shook his head. And then, as slowly and as carefully as he could, he spoke three words. But they were mere sounds, with no more sense than the grunting of a pig.

I said, "I don't know what you're telling me."

He nearly howled with frustration. Then he swept the dirt clear of my writing, and with a finger long and bony he drew a stick figure.

It was bent forward, running furiously. Eli added a round head, a gaping mouth and startled, widened eyes. He jabbed his finger at the running man, then poked me in the ribs. And he spoke again, those horrible groans. Three words.

"Run for it?" I asked. "Run for it?"

Eli shook his head even more violently than before. He brushed away his picture and started over.

And a shadow fell across us.

"He has pudding for brains," said Simon Mawgan, standing square in the doorway. "You won't get anywhere with him."

Eli fell back as though the words had struck him like cannonballs. He groveled for the blankets and at the same time erased the picture on the ground.

"Come up to the house," said Mawgan to me. "You're only wasting time in here."

I followed behind him, leaving Eli alone with the ponies.

We sat at opposite ends of the big table, and Mawgan glared down at his hands. Mary came in from the kitchen and set down three plates. Mawgan drummed his fingers in the silence.

Mary brought forks and knives. She gave me a little, secret smile, then slipped out again.

I coughed. "Thank you for the clothes. They fit well."

Mawgan grunted.

"I'll give them back," I said, "when mine—"

"Keep them." He kept his head lowered. "The fellow before you has no need of them now."

I knew what that meant, and I looked at him as he sat quietly thinking, his face stern, his brow wrinkled. Was he really so kindly as Mary thought? His big hands fiddled with his plate, but he kept silent, and the only sounds came from Mary in the kitchen. I heard her lift the lid of the firebox, the little clang as she moved it aside. I even heard the crackle of flames inside, the slither of coals as she dropped in another scoop.

"Do you know what a sinkhole is?" asked Mawgan suddenly. " 'Course you do. The land around here is riddled with them, John. Sinkholes and mine shafts."

"Yes, sir," I said.

"Fall in one of those and you break your pony's leg. Likely your own neck as well."

"Oh, Uncle," said Mary. She poked her head around the door. "I was with him all the time. I know where the holes are."

"Doesn't matter," said Mawgan. "You stay on the roads from now on. You hear me?"

"Yes, Uncle."

"And no more racing across the moor. Your mother would turn in her grave if she saw the way you carry on."

"Yes, Uncle," said Mary. With a wink at me, she slipped back to the kitchen.

Mawgan joined his hands and rested them on the table edge. And he sat like that, silent as a stone, until Mary arrived—beaming ear to ear—with a covered dish that she put with a flourish in the middle of the table.

"And what's this?" asked Mawgan.

"It's"—she lifted the lid—"starry-gazy!"

There were even more pilchards than last time, their poor blackened heads poking from the crust, watching me balefully with round, dead eyes. And I thought right away of Tommy Colwyn, caught on the moor with a spade in his hands and a row of bodies not quite buried.

"Prettiest thing I've ever seen," said Mawgan. "But look at that, then: You're giving half the pie to young John."

"Oh, there's plenty for you," said Mary, her whole face turning scarlet.

I couldn't have eaten a bite of that pie if it hadn't been for Mary. She sat and watched me tackle each mouthful, smiling and nodding as though I was a baby she was feeding. While I choked down my share a swallow at a time, Simon Mawgan worked at his like a coal miner wielding shovel and pick.

When we were finished, Mawgan took a pipe to one of the big captain's chairs. He arranged himself in the last of the evening sun and filled his pipe with pinches of shredded tobacco. Then he looked up to see if I was watching, and from a bowl at his elbow he took a small piece of glass. He held it up in his fingers.

"Have you seen one of these, John?" he asked.

"No," I said. It was a tube of thin glass, the width of a pencil and closed at both ends. The bowl was full of them—little cylinders with rolls of paper inside.

"Look close, then," said Mawgan, and I leaned forward. "Closer, lad."

With a flourish, Mawgan rapped the tube on the edge of the table. It shattered, scattering glass. And in the instant, the thing burst into flame.

I pulled back—it had nearly set my hair alight—and Mawgan laughed delightedly. It was the paper burning, with a furious flame and a stench of sulfur. He held it to the bowl of his pipe, puffing smoke like a dragon.

"A phosphorus candle." He held it until the flame dwindled, then tossed it into a brass pot on the floor. It fell with a tinkle of glass. "Straight from France, that is, and the first to reach England, I daresay. Take one, lad. Take one."

I stepped forward and helped myself from the bowl. The floor around him was gritty with tiny bits of glass.

"The paper's coated with phosphorus," said Mawgan. "Burns like the devil and nothing puts it out. But the best thing about them"—he tapped the pipestem on his teeth—"is the fact that they float, you see."

Mary brought a candle and walked through the room lighting lamps and tallow dips. The faint, fizzly smell of the phosphorus vanished in a reek of fish oil. Nowhere had I seen so many lamps. There was no need to carry one from room to room, as I would in London; they filled the house with a glow of yellow light.

Mawgan laughed. He was in a fine humor now. "Everything should float," he said. "Wouldn't it be all the easier, hmmm, if gold could float?" Then he sat back, blowing smoke rings that floated like wreaths to the ceiling. He took the pipe from his lips and picked off a piece of tobacco.

"So," he said to me. "What's this I hear about your father?" I must have blanched, and he laughed. "Don't look so shocked, lad. Mary told me everything."

I saw her shoulders twitch, but she didn't look back. She was carrying her candle from one light to the next, guarding the flame with her hand.

"So he's alive, is he?" asked Mawgan.

"Yes," I said.

"Yet you told me there was nobody else. I asked you outright, and you said it straight to my face."

"I told you there was no one I *saw*." I blushed at this, the weakness of it.

"So," said Mawgan. He tamped the tobacco in his pipe. "You were going to let your father perish in some lonely prison rather than worry yourself about it?"

I turned the match end over end in my hands. "That's not the way it was."

"Oh, but that's just how it was. You lied to me, John."

"I had to," I said. "Stumps—"

"That won't do, my son. I give you safety, clothing, I give you food and shelter. Yet you repay me with lies. Why, boy? Why?"

It was Mary who answered. "He didn't know that he could trust you, Uncle. And is that such a wonder?" She snuffed the candle between her fingers. "His shipmates are dead, his father's a prisoner, and how should he know whom to trust?"

Mawgan blew a perfect ring of smoke that drifted up and hovered over him like a halo. He nodded. "Right you are, Mary. Right you are."

I found it hard to believe that this was the same man I'd seen only hours before, livid with rage as he lashed at Eli with a riding crop. Now he sat like a saint, with a charming smile. And I still didn't know whether to trust him or not. He seemed quite harmless, yet every man in Pendennis obeyed his commands.

Mary blew out her candle. "I thought you could help him," she said. "Or I would have kept quiet."

"I understand," said Mawgan. "But you haven't told anyone else, have you?"

"Of course not," said Mary.

"No one at all?"

"Uncle, please."

" 'Course you haven't." Mawgan smiled his gentle smile. "But the problem, you see, is what can I do?"

"Why, ride to Polruan," said Mary. "Bring the coast guard. Bring the excise men."

"Oh, I wish I could, Mary." Mawgan turned to me, and his smile was gone. "But it's not so simple as that, is it then, John?"

"It's not?" I said.

His face turned dark and angry. "Don't play me for a fool, my boy; I'm not a Bristol boatsman. This is your father we're speaking about."

"Really," I said. "I don't know—"

"Lies, lies, lies. You're just full of them, aren't you?"

"Uncle!" cried Mary.

Mawgan tapped out his pipe on his palm. There was still redness in the ashes, but he ground them between his hands. "Tell her," he said. "Tell her what you had in those barrels on the *Isle of Skye*."

"Wine," I said.

"Liar!" Mawgan slammed his fist on the table. "Don't tell me your traveler's tales. Do you think I don't know?"

"What, then?" said Mary, with the same shrill of anger.

"Watch your tongue, girl."

Mawgan sat in his chair like a crouched lion, breathing softly and watching me with eyes that had the yellow glow of the lamps in them. "Tell us," he said, and his voice was soft, but barely so, like porridge about to boil. "Tell us about the night you loaded this wine."

Chapter 8
THE MYSTERY OF
THE BARRELS

" We anchored after dark," I said. "In a little cove. When we lowered the boats, and the men clambered into them, Father held me aside. He told me to stay on the ship."

Mawgan narrowed his eyes. "And you didn't wonder at that?"

"I had no reason to wonder," I said. "He told me to help stow the barrels below."

"Fair enough," said Mawgan. "Go on, then."

He leaned forward, Mary beside him, and I told them as carefully as I could every detail of our strange midnight visit to Spain.

My first glimpse of the shore had come at dawn. Through the morning we bore down on it. And then, a league or so from land, Father had the ship heave to. He went below with the captain and old Cridge, and when he sent for me an hour later to bring them a bottle and

glasses, they were huddled around the table, over a chart I couldn't see. "Why are we waiting?" I asked. The men looked at each other. Captain Stafford had his arms crossed. He didn't look happy at all; he sat there like a bulk of timber. And then Father said, "For nightfall, of course. They'll light a beacon for us, to show us the way." "Aye," said Cridge. "That's right." Then he'd sent me off with a wink.

Simon Mawgan frowned. "And that didn't sound odd?" he asked.

"Not to me," I said. "Remember, this was all new to me. I'd never been to sea before."

As the sun was setting, we'd backed the jibs and swung back toward the land. There was a breeze warmed by the desert, and the men worked bare-chested to set the topsails. That was all, only the topsails. And we ghosted down as the night thickened around us. It was a black night in the dark of the moon, but we showed no lights. I did wonder at that; it was because of pirates, said Father—"The waters here are thick with pirates." But he sent me aloft, up to the foretop with a hooded lantern. And he said, "When I give you the word, show the light at the shore. Count to five and then close it. Do that twice, you understand?" I told him I did. "That's our signal," he said. "So they know we've come on honest business." And up I'd gone into the rigging.

This time it was Mary who scowled. "Even I would have been suspicious at that," she said.

"So I was," I told her.

But it all had been so wonderfully mysterious. The brig slipped through the water in total silence, charged with a sense of danger that tingled in the air like a lightning storm. I watched for pirates, and saw them on every quarter—dark shadows of boats that changed, every one, to wave tops and ripples when I looked more closely. Then, straight ahead and low on the water, I saw a flare of bright light. And Father called up, "Show the lantern!" I opened the shutters, and everything around me—the mast and the stays, the swell of the topsail—glared with a golden glow. The shutters clicked shut, opened again, and when I hooded the lamp for the last time, I could still see the ropes and the rigging burning and moving in my eyes. "Let go!" called a voice, and the anchor fell with a splash, the chain rumbling out. The sound echoed back from a shore I couldn't see as the *Isle of Skye* turned slowly, head to wind. And the topmen—poor Danny Riggins leading them all—came swarming up to furl the sails. Then the boats were swung out and lowered, and I watched them carry my father into the night.

"Did you hear voices?" asked Mawgan. "Any sounds from shore?"

"No," I said. "We must have been at least half a mile off. It took the boats nearly an hour to come back."

We'd listened for them. Every man remaining on the ship stood at the rail, watching and waiting. We were a little world in the darkness, the ship silent, the foresails lying in heaps at the foot of the stays. Old Cridge judged his time by the stars; he kept glancing up. Then we heard it, very faint, the creaking of oars. "Show your light," said Cridge, and I cracked open the shutters. The boats came sliding out of the gloom, each weighted to the gunwales with a stack of barrels. The men in them were grim and quiet, not at all the usual thing when sailors and wine are sitting so close. The barrels came aboard; the boats went off again. And they made four trips before the work was done.

Mawgan nodded. "Forty barrels in all. More or less."

Each in its turn, the boats were hooked onto the tackles and brought aboard. The topsails were unfurled and sheeted home, the foresails raised. They flapped in the wind, and the topsails bellied back against the masts. In silence, the men tramped round the capstan; no chanteys were sung as we left that place. The anchor came up streaming mud and weeds. We made sternway with the helm over; then Cridge ordered the topsail yards braced around, the jibs sheeted home, and we slewed off onto a starboard tack. At the first sign of dawn, we were farther off than we'd been at dusk.

"Is that all that happened?" asked Mawgan.

"It is."

He took a breath. It reminded me of the way the wind lulled before a furious gust. He rapped his fingers on the arm of his chair. They sounded like soldiers marching.

"Now I'll ask you again," he said. "And for the very last time. What exactly did you bring in those barrels, boy?"

"Wine," said I.

Mawgan snorted. "Oh, there was wine in them, true

enough. Yes, and nothing but wine in a third of them. Maybe a flagon or two in each of the rest!"

"A flagon?" I said.

"Aye. Quite enough to satisfy any curious guardsman who tapped a bung, wasn't it? And under the false bottom, packed in sawdust so it wouldn't knock about, was a bar of gold, perhaps? A packet of diamonds?"

"No!" I said.

Simon Mawgan leapt to his feet. He toppled that big, heavy chair as easily as a bottle. He meant to hit me—I was sure of it—but Mary ran between us.

"Look at him," she said, her hands on his chest. "Just look at him, Uncle. You can see he edn't lying."

I must have stood there ghastly white, my fingers fiddling with the little glass match that Mawgan had given me. Suddenly it all made sense: a mysterious night on a dark shore; sawdust in the bilge of the *Skye;* the wreckers' obsession with a few broken barrels. There seemed to be only one explanation, and Mawgan had led me to it step by step. But still I couldn't believe it.

I shook my head. "It's not true. You're wrong about this."

"I think not," said Mawgan, a grim smile on his lips. "It is true. And I'm afraid there's no help for you anywhere now."

Mary whirled around to face me, then just as abruptly turned back to her uncle. "What's true?" she said. "I don't understand!"

"The barrels," said Mawgan. He was talking not to her

but to me. "He was hiding something in the barrels, boy. Your father's a smuggler."

"He's not!" I said.

It couldn't be true. Father a smuggler? No, it wasn't possible. I'd seen him follow every law and every rule, cheating no one of so much as a farthing. Ever since I could remember, he'd drummed into me the importance of honest work. A duty, he'd called it: "It's the duty of man to earn his living by harming no soul."

But the sawdust . . . how had it gotten into the bilge of the *Skye* and clogged the pumps if it didn't come from the barrels?

Father had built up his business from nothing. He started as a petty clerk, and in a few short years came to own a fine house and two ships and a carriage and . . .

How had he done that? I'd never wondered before. And if he *was* a smuggler, what better way to smuggle gold—or anything else—than to roll it right past the eyes of the excise men in false-bottomed barrels, avoiding all taxes and duty? But Father wouldn't do that; it made no sense.

Then why did we load the barrels at night? *Skulking about like thieves.*

Mawgan watched these thoughts passing, in frowns and teary eyes, across my face. Then he touched me gently on the arm. "Well, come, come. Don't look so downhearted, lad. Your father's not the first smuggler, nor the last, I'm sure. Nothing wrong with a bit of smuggling, the way the taxes are these days."

The coast was rife with smugglers, it was true. Only a brave man poked about the shore on a moonless night. But my father? He liked to boast that every drop of tea he ever drank had the duty paid. So if Mawgan was right, then Father's whole life had been a sham and a farce. If Mawgan was right, then greed had wrecked the *Isle of Skye*. And greed had put us on the same side of the law as the wreckers.

"So what happened to it?" asked Mawgan suddenly.

"To what?" I asked.

"To the gold, boy! To the gold. Or whatever it was." The anger was building in him again, darkening his face like a squall. "You passed Gibraltar, did you not?"

"Yes." It had been dusk, and an English squadron had been making for the harbor.

"And then you turned north," said Mawgan. "And sometime between there and the Channel, someone shifted it—didn't they?—from the barrels to a different place. The bilge, I would bet."

"But Uncle," cried Mary. "You said that—"

"Sawdust!" snapped Mawgan. "That's all there was. Tobacco would have floated. So would tea or coffee, chocolate or bottles of gin; even sugar or salt would have floated in their packets. But gold would still be there—wouldn't it?—lying out on the Tombstones."

He was breathing heavily. I found myself squeezing my glass match so hard that it could have broken in my fist. I slipped it in my pocket and held out empty hands. "I don't know what was in the barrels," I said. "Whatever it was is gone forever."

"Not quite," said Mawgan. "Because your father will know where it is."

The truth of this stunned me. If Caleb Stratton thought there might be gold—or anything else—on the Tombstones, he would get it. If not from my father, then from me. I doubted that he would sit and listen, as Mawgan had done, to my story. And then another thought formed, and swirled in my mind like troubled water. Was this why Mawgan had saved me? To find for himself the secret of the false-bottomed barrels?

"For myself, of course, I don't care about the gold," said Mawgan, as though he'd read these thoughts in my mind. "But the wreckmen are talking about it, John. From the night on the Tombstones, when barrels came ashore broken and spilling sawdust, they've been thinking on this. Your father's the key. If Stumps knows of it—"

"He does." I told Mawgan what Stumps had said: *I'm that close to having more gold than I've ever dreamed of. A passage up the coast, one night at sea.*

"And straight to Execution Dock," said Mawgan. "That's my guess. He'll take the gold and sell your father for a nice reward. But if Caleb Stratton finds him first . . . Well, let's say he'd better not."

"For heaven's sake," said Mary. "Just talk to Stumps. Offer him money, and he'll—"

"Can't do that," said Mawgan flatly.

"Why not?"

"Because Stumps has vanished. He hasn't been seen at the blockhouse or anywhere else."

Mawgan sat back with the smug smile of a cat. He seemed almost happy at this new twist in my fate, whistling the notes of an odd little song as he took up his pipe and tobacco.

Mary drew her legs up on her chair and sat on her ankles. "Uncle?" she asked. "Why were you looking for Stumps?"

"What?" he said. A big pinch of tobacco hovered over his pipe. He stuffed it in, then pressed it down with his thumb. "I don't care for your tone, Mary. I have no business with Stumps. If you must know, I was taking tea today with Parson Tweed. This is the talk in the village."

"And what has happened to Stumps?"

"I have no idea. My guess is he's hiding. Waiting for the moon." Mawgan cracked another of the matches, scattering more glass around his chair. He lit his pipe and stared at Mary through a cloud of thick smoke. "Or are you suggesting that I know more about this than I've told you?"

"Of course not," said Mary.

"Good. Now let me sit here and think."

We left Mawgan at the table, in his haze of sweet smoke, and went outside, Mary and I. It was a warm night, quiet in the valley, with not a breath of wind in the hedges, though high, shredded clouds oozed like ink stains across the stars. A little bite of moon seemed to balance on the rooftop, and then rose as I watched, as though leaping from there to start its flight across the sky.

"The wreckers will be watching tonight," said Mary.

"It seems calm enough," I said.

"Here it does, yes. But along the cliffs, with the clouds coming in, there could be killing by dawn."

She said it sadly, in a low voice that was almost a whisper. "I'm ready," she said. "If it comes to that."

I took her arm, and we walked by the front of the house. In the window, I could see Simon Mawgan puffing on his pipe.

"Can he really help me?" I asked.

"He'll do what he can," said Mary. We walked through the square of light that fell from the window, then down the long side of the house. "Uncle Simon gets angry sometimes, but he's just as quick to forget."

"I saw him take a riding crop to Eli."

Mary scuffed her feet in the grass. "I've seen that, too. Uncle gets in a rage at Eli, but he never harms him."

"He was trying to tell me something," I said. "Eli was. He drew a picture, like this." I took her to the cart path and there, in the dirt of the ruts, I sketched the running man with my finger. "I think he was trying to warn me."

"Warn you of what?"

"I don't know."

Mary peered at my drawing. "Oh, John, that means nothing," she said. "That's the man on the tomb."

I didn't understand.

"Come and I'll show you."

We kept walking, beyond the house, between the stable and the cottage, all its windows dark. "You have to realize," she said. "You don't know the stories. You don't know what's happened before." Her face was pale in the moonlight, and I could see she was trying to decide what to say, or how to say it.

We left the buildings behind before she spoke again. "They've been like this ever since I can remember. Eli despises Uncle Simon."

"Then why does your uncle keep him here?"

Mary looked puzzled. "He can't run him off."

"Because he's so old?"

"He's not so old," said Mary. "Why, he's only a year or two older than Uncle Simon. When I was very small I couldn't tell them apart. Now you'd never guess they're brothers, would you?"

"Brothers?" I said.

"Yes. He's my uncle Eli, though I never called him that. He's always been Eli. Plain old Eli. And all this land is half his."

We passed through the hedgerows and started up the slope of the valley. We were heading north, away from the sea. "Then why," I asked, "does he live in that little cottage?"

"Years ago, they both did. Oh, once the Mawgans had a lovely place, but they lost that in a fire. When the wrecking started, Uncle Simon built the new house on the ruins of the old one. Eli is the only man I know who never touched a thing from the wrecks. He worked in the ground, in the mines, for his shilling a day. He called it honest work; you can see what it did to him."

I said, "He didn't lose his tongue in the mines."

"No. Eli despised the wrecking so much that one night he rode to Polruan in a storm. The wreckers had a ship embayed; they didn't see him go. Like the wind he went, and he came back at dawn with the revenue men. They were an hour too late. The wreck was stripped, but in the moor they found a fresh grave. There was one man hanged for that—Caleb's brother."

Near the top of the slope, the ground steepened. Mary panted as she climbed—it didn't occur to me that she might be crying. And at the top we felt the wind again. It rushed at us over the moor, it came with a dry moan through the grass. And I heard a thrumming, a faint beat, that was surf on the cliffs.

Mary stepped along the ridge, and the wind took her hair and her clothes and stretched them like streamers. "The wreckers held a court; they do everything proper. If Eli hadn't been a Mawgan, if he hadn't shared right of wreck, they would have killed him on the spot."

"So they cut out his tongue?" I said.

She turned round, and we stood for a moment with the wind at our sides. "That's why I have to stop this," she said. "However I can."

She looked at me as though waiting, wanting me to promise to help. And when I didn't—I couldn't do that—she pulled away. "Come on. We're almost there."

We ran east for a way, then back down the slope, to a jumble of enormous stones arranged on the moor. Four stood upright, like the walls of a shack, and the roof was an enormous slab lying at a tilt across them. In the eerie light of cloud-shadowed stars, it looked ancient and foreboding.

"It's a cromlech," said Mary. "It's the tomb."

"Whose?" I said.

"Nobody knows."

The stones didn't join. There were rocks heaped at the corners, but wind moaned through the gaps. We walked toward it, then in a circle round it. In a corner was an opening, a dark, gaping hole where the stacked rocks had tumbled away.

"What's in there?" I asked.

"Nothing. Only dirt."

"I want to see." But when I stepped up on the rocks, Mary pulled me down.

"Don't!" she said. "Uncle Simon says there's a terrible curse. He says anyone who even looks in there will die within the day."

I laughed. "You believe that?"

"Yes. Yes, I do," said Mary. "But see, John? There's carvings on the stone. Here's your running man."

Even in the darkness I could see it easily. The lines were deeply carved, and I traced them with my fingers, up the legs and the body, round the head. I felt foolish. Eli hadn't told me to run for it; he'd said, "Running man."

"But why?" I asked Mary. "Why did he show me this?"

"I don't know," she said. "You can't always tell with Eli."

The stone was cool and gritty. I kept following the lines of the drawing, hoping to feel in them the secret that Eli was trying to pass on. A gust of wind whistled in the stone, like voices inside. Mary shivered.

And a sound came to us, a hollow pop, then another.

"Gunshots," I said.

"Wait," said Mary. She clutched my arm and listened. I could see every muscle in her neck, and her eyes were staring. "Only two," she breathed. "Thank God, only two."

"What does it mean?" I asked.

Her skirts billowed like sails as the wind gusted again. "There's a ship in the bay."

Chapter 9
A SHIP EMBAYED

*I*climbed up onto the top of the cromlech, onto the thick stone roof of the tomb. I stared into the wind until my eyes stung, but I could see no sign of a ship.

"We're too far from the sea," said Mary. She wouldn't climb up; she stood off a few yards, only a shadow at the edge of the darkness.

"I might see her topsails," I said. "Topgallants if she's big enough." They would rise above the cliffs like huge, floating birds.

"It's too far!"

"Not if she's right at the cliffs. She might be aground."

"No!" said Mary. "Only two shots. Three is a ship coming ashore. Four is a wreck." In the wind, her voice was faint and high, the voice of a small girl. "John, hurry!"

I turned to leave. And in the action, the turning away, I saw the sail.

"There she is!" I cried. It took shape to the south, a tier

89

of canvas like a stack of child's blocks. Topsails and topgallants and royals. A full-rigged ship. "Mary, come look."

But she wouldn't come closer. I tried to fix a bearing on it, a course from the house. Then I scrambled down from the slab. And Mary was gone.

"Mary!" I shouted.

"Here!" she said. "Hurry."

I couldn't see her. I followed the sound, over the brow of the knoll, into the gloom of the valley. "Hurry!" she said, and I ran straight down the slope. But I'd gone only a dozen steps when a hand grabbed my ankle and I tumbled to the ground.

I cried out.

"Shhh! Someone's coming," said Mary.

It was a man on a horse, and he rode at a gallop the same way we'd come. A dark shape on the moor, then a silhouette on the ridge, he came with a snorting and a hammer of hooves. Across the sky he rode, a black thing tattered and torn, a cape flowing back. Straight to the cromlech, to that ancient stone tomb.

The horse reared up, and he slid from its back to the ground. I felt Mary's arm fall across my shoulder as she pushed me down in the grass.

"He mustn't see us," she whispered.

"Who is it?"

"I think it's— I can't really tell."

The horse was between us and the rider. We could see the man's legs below its belly, nothing more than that. He strode to the cromlech and climbed up the loose stack of rocks.

"He's going inside," I said.

"No one," said Mary, "would dare go in there."

The horse lowered its head and nibbled at the grass. It stepped forward, reins swinging loose. Only one step, and it went no farther.

We could hear a clattering sound, metal on metal. Then the grinding of boots tramping on stone. And a gust of wind howled through the cromlech like the cries of lost souls.

In a moment the man reappeared. But still we could see no more than his legs, until he came right to the horse and climbed up in the saddle. And then he was like a silvery trace, like a thing not quite there. He was holding something bulky and square, and he balanced it before him as he grabbed up the reins and put his heels to the horse. He swung it round.

"Can you see who it is?" I asked.

"I can't be sure," said Mary. "But it looks like Uncle Simon."

Whoever it was, he rode off even faster than he'd come, over the knoll and straight to the south, to the sea.

"Come on!" said Mary. But I was already on my feet. And when we ran off in different directions, we both stopped and looked back in surprise.

"Where are you going?" she asked.

"To the cromlech," I said.

"Why?"

"We have to see what's inside."

Mary was horrified. "You can't go in there," she said.

"We have to see."

I started up, and she came at my heels. "Please, John. It's cursed. Go in there and you'll die."

I kept walking. Even when Mary grabbed me I kept going. She fell on the ground behind me, pleading, reaching with her hand. But I went straight to the cromlech, and straight inside.

The wind whirled through the tomb. And a strange green glow came from the walls, from the lichen that grew there—eerie patches of light that seemed like eyes in the darkness. I imagined the stones were watching me as I fumbled to the back of the tomb, and found what I knew would be there. They were stacked in a pile, and I took up the closest and shoved it out before me. I heard it rattle down the stones, and when I came out Mary was holding it.

"There," said I. "That's what Eli sent me to find."

"A lantern," she said.

"A beacon," I told her.

We ran to the house with the lantern between us, each with a hand on the bail. It rocked, making the shutters open and close, and the thing tolled like a bell.

The stable door was open, but we passed it by. We dropped the lantern on the porch and crashed through the door. Mary called out for her uncle. But the place was empty. And when we looked in the stable, the black horse was missing.

"It couldn't have been him," said Mary. "It couldn't be Uncle Simon."

"Then where is he?" I said.

"I don't know. But I'm going to find out."

We bridled the ponies and rode south at a steady pace, up and down the humps of the moor. Before we came to the road, on the last rise of the moor, we turned to the west. And there at our side was the ship.

She was a ghost in the dark, beating hard to windward with every sail set. Each mast was a tower, tapering from courses to royals, each yard braced back to the shrouds. Between them stretched the staysails, a wall of canvas. She leaned in the wind and hurled herself through the waves in a blizzard of spindrift. And I would have given my soul to be aboard her.

It was a beautiful, ghastly scene, all in black and shades of gray. To the west was Wrinkle Head, to the east lay Northground, and between them was a vast bay with the ship in the middle. She bore down on Wrinkle Head, taking each wave on the bow with a blast of spray.

Along the cliffs there were people, forty or more, some tall and some short, thin ones and plump ones, children and men and old women. They stood at the edge like crows on a roof ridge, watching the ship on the sea.

Pressed by the wind, beaten by waves, the ship slipped sideways a yard for every ten she gained. The big mainsail disappeared, seeming to shrink up into the foot of the topsail. And then the bow swung round to the wind. Staysails and jibs shivered like flags. The yards went crashing across. The ship slowed as she turned, coming upright into the wind, then raced off toward Northground, toward the other wall of her prison.

From the cliffs came a groan, a cry of despair. A tall man raised his fist, and shook it at the ship. And then, as one, the rabble shouldered axes and pikes and followed the ship in a long, wavering line.

I looked for Simon Mawgan among them. But there was no sign of him, no sign of his horse. Not a man in the group carried a lantern.

As they walked below us they started singing, first one and then all—men, women, and children—their voices swelling into a slow and mournful hymn.

> Hear me, O God,
> As I pray to Thee,
> From the shore
> Of the perilous sea.
> If sailors there are,
> And wrecks there must be,
> I beseech You
> To send them to me.
> I beseech You
> To send them to me.

Mary clucked at her pony and backed it over the rise. Mine went with it, as though they were lashed together. We hobbled them out of sight from the cliffs, then crawled down to the shelter of Mary's garden.

There was nothing we could do but let the scene unfold; the ship would clear the cape, or she would not. For her, the wind was like a slope of shifting sand, and for every yard she climbed, she slipped a little back. For an hour or more she ran toward the cape, inching up the slope of wind, until she was no more than a shadow in the distance.

Then she turned again, and the wreckers cheered; the ship was still embayed.

"Sometimes this lasts for days," said Mary. "The people wander back and forth and back and forth. They sleep up here, and never leave until it's over, until the ship is free or on the rocks. There edn't a one of them who'll go away and miss the chance to be first at a wreck."

It seemed an awful thing to do, as cruel as the crowds that massed in their fine clothes for a London hanging.

"So you see what I mean," said Mary. "They're waiting, is all. They're not using false lights."

"Where's the man from the cromlech?" I asked. "Where's your uncle?"

Mary shrugged. "But he edn't here, is he?"

To me, that only meant he was waiting somewhere else, ready with his lantern. He would wait till dawn and then no more; his was a nighttime business. Once the ship had seen the shore, there would be no use for beacons.

The ship sailed past, and past again, trapped between the capes. And then, when the night was nearly done, the Widow came, standing in her wagon with her hands upon the shoulders of her small and dusty driver. She called out to her horses with a wildly piercing cry, and they pounded on before her with their heads outthrust, their coats ashine with sweat.

"Now the ship is doomed," said Mary. "When the Widow arrives, there's a wreck in the offing. She feels it like a coming storm."

"Where has she come from?" I asked.

"From the moors. She lives in a house flung together

from wood and thatch, down at the end of the Mawgan land."

"You've been there?"

"I've seen it," said Mary. "Uncle Simon takes her food sometimes. Tea and loaves of bread. And I've seen Eli shuffling off that way all by himself as night is coming down. But in the whole village there edn't another man who'll ride out to the Widow's place."

She passed below us, the horses slowing as she whistled to them.

"I followed Uncle Simon once," said Mary. "I watched him go up to the house. But the Widow wouldn't come to the door. I saw her face in the window—it looked like frost on the glass—and she never moved from there."

"And her driver?"

"That's Simple Tom. The idjit boy. He used to wander through the village, until the Widow took him in. Won't talk to another soul; only to her."

Once more the ship scudded past, close-hauled for the point. Once more she turned away. In my heart and mind, I was sailing with her. Though she moved in silence, like a toy on the water, I heard inside me the awful creaking of her planks and the strain of the lines; I felt the icy blasts of tossed spray. And I felt the danger, that horrible thrill of peril.

Behind her came the wreckers. And at last they tired of their trekking. They settled down round the Widow's wagon, and soon others came up from the road with bundles of wood and tarpaulins. They built a fire that filled the wind with sparks, with a tang of smoke that drifted down right upon us.

"The whole village is here," I said.

"I daresay it is," said Mary.

"Then Pendennis is empty?"

"Yes."

I looked away. "I'm going there. I'm going to look for my father."

I thought she would stop me, or at least try. Really, I hoped she would. But she only said, "We'll both go."

"But if they find me—"

"They won't," said Mary. She got up into a crouch and started picking at her flowers, breaking off the heads. "I know every street and passageway."

I didn't argue; I didn't want to. Mary took the flowers in her hand, and together we slipped back to the ponies and rode off for the village.

Side by side we trotted down toward the stone bridge. With the headlands behind us, we could see the buildings of Pendennis stepped on the slopes of the harbor's far shore. Scattered through its length, a few little windows shone with lamplight. But it was a dark place. And it filled me with fear.

Chapter 10

WRAPPED IN CHAINS

*T*he hooves of our ponies clopped on the bridge. We climbed up the high road and entered the village through a break in an ancient wall. And there we left the ponies, at a public trough where water trickled from a spout shaped like a fish head.

Mary took me first to the churchyard. "I never come to the village without stopping here," she said.

The wind sighed past the church and blew in whirls round the headstones. The stained-glass saints glowed with a faint light, as though they watched us—or watched the storm—through a veil of thin curtains. Behind them moved a shape, and Parson Tweed went gliding by the row of faces.

Mary took a flower from her bunch and laid it down by a headstone. "For my father," she said. She left the second on the grave beside it. "For my mother." She tucked back her hair. "I bring flowers for the people who mean much to me," she said. "For my heroes. You don't think that's silly, do you?"

"No," I said.

She left four more—for her aunt and for Peter, for a friend and a cousin—and still kept one in her hand as we walked toward the gate.

"Who's that for?" I asked.

Mary smiled. She pressed the flower into my hand. "For you."

She meant it kindly. But to be counted among her dead heroes, to be honored the same way at the side of their graves, gave me an icy chill.

"What's the matter?" asked Mary.

I was wondering: The next time Mary came to the churchyard, would she be stooping at *my* grave as well? With a shudder, I thought of the cromlech. *It's cursed. Go in there and you'll die.*

The wind chased us round the back of the church as we headed down to the harbor. Mary didn't look back. She started off along a lane, knowing I would follow. I shoved her flower into the breast of my jersey. The others were already scattering across the graves, rolling and spinning from stone to stone.

From the dirt to cobblestones, we traced the route I'd ridden with Simon Mawgan. We arrived at the harborfront not far from the same spot where he'd found me in the hands of Caleb Stratton, a knife at my throat. But now the tide was high, and the boats that had lain stranded in the mud tugged like horses at their mooring ropes, rubbing against the seawall with a squeal of cork.

The long street was dark and empty. In both directions, the buildings crowded around us, inns and warehouses and deserted boatworks. My father could be in any one of them — or none at all. It seemed an impossible quest.

Even Mary looked downhearted. "Did Stumps give you a clue?" she asked. "Anything at all?"

I tried to remember. And I heard again that awful, quiet rasping of his voice. *If you put the wreckmen on me, your father will rot where he lies. Only I know where he is, and there he'll stay.* But there was no more than that, no hint at all.

"Is there a song that he knows?" asked Mary.

"Stumps?" I asked.

"Your father, silly," she said. "Is there a tune you can whistle, and your father will know that it's you?"

"Yes," I said. When my mother lay dying, there was a song he'd sung to comfort her. He sat by her bed, and held her hand, and sang it over and over from dark until dawn. "I don't know the name, but it sounds like this." I whistled it for her.

"Again," said Mary when I'd finished. "Keep whistling. But stop if you see someone. Stop if you hear a sound."

Up the street we walked, and the notes came softly back through the canyon of buildings. They came back through time, and I felt myself six years old again, seeing the horrors of those long nights, my mother's face shrinking like old wax, her pretty face turning awful and ugly.

"Keep whistling," said Mary. We walked inland, the wind behind us, past an inn and a chandlery.

In the end, my mother's teeth had stood out in rows, bared and gumless like those of a horse. And my father, seeing my distress, locked me from the room. I'd sat in the hallway, hearing the song through the door until, one night, it suddenly ended. When the door opened, my father looked down at me. He said—

"Don't stop, John." Mary gave my arm a gentle shake. "If we pass him by, we'll never find him."

I started again, hardly aware I'd stopped at all.

My father had said, "She's gone." I thought he meant that she'd somehow risen from the bed and disappeared. When I looked in and saw her there, covered over with a sheet, I thought he was playing a trick. I'd pulled away the cover and stared down at that—that *thing* that I hardly knew was my mother.

"Shhh!" said Mary. When she squeezed my arm, I jerked with sudden fear. "Someone's coming," she said, and pulled me into a deep doorway.

Footsteps sounded on the cobblestones. Not one person, but two.

We crouched by a wall, in the darkness, and hardly dared look. The people would pass within an arm's length of us.

I could hear Mary breathing. I could hear my own heart, like the whistling flight of an owl. The footsteps grew louder.

Then a peal of laughter, and a woman's voice thick with Cornish brogue. "An' I says to 'im, 'Why,' says I, 'I lost one zackly like that only t'udder day.' An' lissen, Mally; it were jist the same one, jist the same ould roul o' lither! Did'ee ever see or hear tell o' sich a thing?"

They walked right by, two old women laughing and

nodding, leaning on each other like drunken sailors. Their laughter, their footsteps, faded off down the street. And I heard instead the slop and chop of water at a wall.

I sat up. It wasn't a doorway that Mary had led us to, but a narrow alley roofed by the top floor of the chandlery: a passageway to the sea. A draft came up it, cold and salty. I whistled my song, and it filled the space like the voices of a choir.

And I heard a scratching in reply.

Mary's fingers squeezed around my arm. Again I whistled; again came the scratching.

"It's coming from the bottom," said Mary.

We walked deeper into the alley. Where the chandlery ended, the floor dropped off into a walled flight of carved steps, narrow and steep. I started down them.

The scratching stopped. I whistled softly. And the same tune came echoing back, the same rhythm tapped out on stone or brick.

With a hand braced on each wall, I felt with my foot for the next step down. Mary pressed behind me, and slowly we descended. At the bottom the steps went straight to the water. On one side the wall was bare plaster. But on the other the building was made of stone, all chipped and cracked. And set in an arch was a small and ancient door. I pushed against it and felt the jar of a heavy bolt.

I pressed my ear to the wood and listened for the tapping. Looking up from the bottom, the alley was like a gun muzzle, a dark tunnel with a small, square slot for the entrance. The tapping echoed through it, but I couldn't hear it at the door.

"The harbor," said Mary. She had her eyes closed. "It's coming from the harbor."

I moved to the bottom step, with the water at my feet. I poked my head out into the wind. A narrow wooden ledge jutted from the building, a tarred timber just four inches wide. Above it was a drain tunnel, an enormous pipe made of brick. Green water thick as paste oozed from its mouth. Things like soft icicles hung from the brick, swaying like pendulums. And the tapping came from there.

"Father!" I called. "Father, it's John."

His answer was a mumble, like the frantic sounds of old Eli, and my first thought was that Stumps had done the same thing to my father. And then I remembered. *His lips will look like splattered worms, and he'll choke on his very own tongue.*

I pulled myself back into the passageway. "He's in there," I said. "In the drain."

"Are you going in?"

"Yes."

Mary touched the bolted door. "This building was once a brewery," she said. "You should be able to come out this way."

I took off my coat and spread it on the steps. "We'll need the ponies, Mary. Could you get them?"

"All right." She started to leave, then stopped. "Be careful," she said, and went running up the steps.

The stone was broken at the corner. Clumps of grass and bushy plants grew in the chinks where mortar had fallen away. As I felt for handholds huge pieces came loose in my hand. They clattered down and fell with a splash into the dark water of the harbor. I swung out and planted my feet on the narrow, slippery ledge.

The water was just a few feet below, an ebb tide swirling round the stone. I couldn't swim. If I fell in there, I'd be swept out to sea like a bit of wood.

Spread-eagled, groping for holds, I inched along the wall like a fly. The water gurgled; the wind's gusts tried to pluck me from the ledge. But I gritted my teeth and kept going. And before long, my hand closed on the lip of the drain tunnel. I slithered through, into a dank and fetid hole. A furtive rustle of rats preceded me.

The space was large enough that I could easily stand. I went only a few steps before I came upon Father. He lay on a ledge of brick, a foot above the slime of the open drain. He was on his back, with an old neckerchief knotted tight in his mouth. I tore it loose, and he gasped long breaths of that foul air.

"John," he said. His voice was hoarse; even the sound was painful. "I can't believe . . . it's really you."

I dipped my fingers in the mire and touched them to his lips. His tongue darted out, fat and pale like a garden slug. "Moved," he said. "Used to lie . . . against the brick. Wet there."

He was right. Water condensed on the walls of the drain—good, clear water that tasted of lime. I pressed my hand against it until a tiny pool filled my palm, then let it dribble into his mouth. He drank handful after handful as the muscles in his throat burbled and creaked. Then I rubbed it on his eyes and his forehead, and in the thick bristles of his beard.

"Better," he said. "Thank you."

"There are ponies coming," I told him. "We have to get you up to the street. Is there another way out?"

"Trapdoor," he said. "Above you."

"What's up there?"

"Nothing," he said. "Empty room."

"Can you walk?"

He shook his head. "I'm changed," is what I thought he said. But as I ran my hands along his legs, feeling for blood or broken bones, I found metal collars locked round his ankles, heavy chains padlocked to ringbolts in the brick. There were more collars at his wrists, another belt of chain around his waist. He was fettered like a dog to his narrow shelf. Even with a file it would take time to work him free; with a hammer and chisel, I would need hours. I had to get the key, and only one man would have it.

"Have you seen Stumps?" I asked.

"Who?"

"The man with no legs. They say he's vanished. They say he's—"

Father rattled the chains. "No!" he said. "Comes at dawn . . . at dark."

"He came today?"

Father nodded.

"At dark he came?"

"Listen." Father stretched his head toward me. "Tomorrow, on the night tide . . . taking me out."

"Stumps?" I asked.

"Yes." His voice hissed through the tunnel. "No . . . no moon . . . leaving by boat."

"Where?"

"God knows," said Father, with a dreadful shudder.

Smuggled gold had led us to this. Gold and greed had wrecked the *Isle of Skye* and killed its crew. In that instant, if it had been anyone but my father lying there, I could have hit him. Hit him and kicked him and punched him for all that he'd done. But I only glared at him in the darkness.

"Help me." With a rumble and clank of chain, he tried to reach me with his hand. I could see his fingers flexing, but I didn't want to hold him. Not then.

Father groaned. "Come at high tide. When he unchains me. Only chance."

We heard footsteps then, hurrying down the steps of the passageway. And Mary's voice, in a hushed call: "John. Come on!"

Father squirmed in the chains. His whole body arched, and fell back, and with white eyes he stared up at me. His hand groped like a claw. And I took it.

"Who's up there?" he asked.

"A friend," I told him. "Don't worry."

He relaxed. He eased back on the dank brick. "You'll come?" he asked.

I squeezed his hand. "Yes."

"Before you go . . . move me to the wall."

I shifted him as best I could, prodding and pushing until he lay on his side with his mouth against the wall. Before I left, I tied the neckerchief back in place, though not as tightly as before. Then I felt for the trapdoor and pushed it open.

It was almost as dark above as it was in the drain. But what little light filtered down was enough to show me a scene that I've tried ever since to forget. In the depths of the drain, in a black huddled mass, the rats were waiting. They'd been gnawing at my father's boot, and the leather on one side was stripped away from heel to toe. And the flesh—it was ghastly pink; they'd started to eat his foot.

Shaken, I lowered the trap. The door to the passageway locked with a simple crossbar. As soon as it opened, Mary was there.

"What's wrong?" she said. "Where's your father?"

"He's wrapped in chains," I said. "We have to come back."

"Is he all right?"

"For now," I said, and pushed the door.

Mary flung herself at it. "Wait!" she cried, and stopped it with her hands. "There must be a latch or something. Some way for Stumps to come and go."

She was right. He'd looped a bit of string around the crossbar and tied it to the bent-over end of a rusted nail set low to the ground. The nail fit loosely in its hole, and by pulling it out we could raise the crossbar.

"It's an old trick," said Mary. "Half the houses in Pendennis use a latchstring."

Daylight was about two hours off when we closed the door and heard the crossbar thunk into place. Already there was a hint of gray in the sky across the harbor. And with the dawn would come Stumps.

I pulled on my coat. We stood looking at the eastern sky when our passage suddenly brightened. I wheeled around. At the top of the steps, in the darkness of the chandlery, was a man with an opened lantern.

Chapter 11

A GARGOYLE COME
TO LIFE

Mary gasped. With the glare from the lantern, we couldn't see the man behind it. He took a step toward us, and the lantern rose at the end of his arm. The light flared across the plastered wall on our left and turned the flight of steps into a grid of black bars.

"Mary, my child?" asked the man.

"Parson Tweed?" said Mary.

"What a start you gave me. What a dreadful start." The light wavered and lowered. "And mercy me, it's Master John. Searching for your father, I daresay."

"Yes," said I.

The parson raised his lantern. The light shone down on his enormous hat, but all the rest of him was shadowed. "And was it a prosperous search?" he asked.

"No," I replied.

He clucked his tongue. "But you'll keep looking, I'm sure."

"Yes, sir."

"As indeed will I. Godspeed, Master John." Then he turned, and the lantern light glinted around the edges of his cassock. Like a figure lit by fire, he walked away from us to the street. "Bless you, my boy," he said, and was gone.

Mary touched my sleeve. "Why did you lie to him?" she whispered.

"I don't want anyone to know where my father is."

"But the parson—"

"No one." I took her hand and started up the stairs. Mary pulled back at first, then followed.

"You've made a mistake," she said, her voice low but urgent. "I've known Parson Tweed all my life. You can trust him. You have to trust someone."

"I do," I said. "I trust you."

Mary had tethered the ponies to a post. They both nudged at her with their noses. "Where do we go?" she asked.

"The blockhouse," I said.

"But that's where Stumps lives."

"It's where he'd keep the keys," I told her.

We left the ponies where they were—I thought of the clatter their hooves would make on the stones—and walked without speaking down the cobbled street. The wind moaned in eaves and chimneys. It gusted around us. I was afraid, and Mary must have felt this, for she took my hand for a moment, and squeezed it in hers. Then we reached the blockhouse and saw its gaping open doorway, and my memories of the place went spinning through my mind.

For a time we only listened. But there were no sounds at all from the building, no movement or breaths. Before my courage could leave me completely, I crouched down and shuffled inside.

Blind in the darkness, I went straight to his shelf. If he was there, it was now he would strike. I felt along the plank, knocking down shells and bits of wood, scattering his sad little treasures. I was in too much of a hurry; I felt the whole plank tip forward, and everything went flying to the floor.

"Hurry," said Mary from outside. "Hurry, John."

I picked things up and threw them aside. Rope quoits, bird feathers, wooden beads, and boat nails. I scrabbled in the loose straw and the dirt. And I found the keys against the wall—a hard ring of iron that felt cold in my fingers. I took it, and I ran, Mary right behind me. Down the street, past the ponies, down the stairs of the passageway. I fumbled for the latchstring. I wrenched open the door. And only when we were safe inside did I breathe again.

Mary was shocked to see my father wedged down in that terrible place, his eyes goggling up at us in sudden fear. The rats squealed and went scurrying up into the elbow of the drain. And when I dropped down, Mary stayed above.

I pulled down the neckerchief, and Father gasped, "John!"

"Keys," I cried, and rattled them. "I got the keys."

"Oh, John," he said. Father was crying.

I tried every key in every lock. Fumbling like a blind man, I pushed them in and turned them. But none opened the locks. And in frustration, I wrenched at those heavy chains.

"No use," said Father. "Only way . . . you have to come when he's here."

I didn't know whether I could bear it, struggling in the darkness with the legless man. I felt the links of chain, the ringbolts at their ends. "A file," I said. "I can maybe get a file."

Father didn't answer. I touched his shoulder and told him to wait, and Mary reached down a hand to help me up. When her face was close to mine, she whispered, "Look." And she took my fingers, and touched them to the curve of the brick at the top of the drain.

Barnacles. They grew in small clusters, rough as gems against my hand. A small shred of dried seaweed came away in my palm.

I saw right away what it meant. Stumps had made sure that no one but he could find the smuggled gold. If he was kept away, if he was killed by the wreckers, the drain would flood on the highest tide—just after the moon. My father would drown, and the secret of the gold would be lost.

I swallowed. "Father," I said, "I'll be back as soon as I can."

Mary stepped aside as I lowered the trap. I did it slowly, but still it made a hollow, ringing thump like the closing of the door to a jail cell. And then we heard the horrible little squeaks—the rats going back to their work.

"Please," said Mary. "Let us get away from here."

The sky glowed with the faint hint of coming day when we climbed again the steps to the street. A few yards away, the ponies snorted and whinnied to see us, their manes tangled by the wind. Mary unhitched hers without a word and jumped up on its back. I could think of almost nothing but my father trapped there in the tunnel, watching the tide rise around him and not knowing when it would stop.

"Please go ahead," said I. "I want a moment to think."

"I understand," said Mary. "I'll wait for you on the high road."

She went off with a slow clop of hooves. I watched her, then pressed my face against the pony's chest and found comfort in the beat of its blood, the rough warmth of its hair. I thought of my father laughing as we stepped from the carriage and saw our ship, the *Isle of Skye*, for the first time. He'd stood gazing at the figurehead, a beautiful woman. And he'd grown sad when I asked who it was. "Your mother," he'd said. He'd hired the finest craftsmen in London to carve and paint it. "Is that what she looked like?" I'd asked. I thought of him walking proudly through his offices, men in cravats bobbing up to smile and wish him good morning. But it was no use; I kept seeing him tearing at the chains until his wrists were raw, fighting and kicking as the water rose inch by inch, up his shoulders and chest, creeping up the arch of his neck, pouring into his nose and his open, screaming mouth.

He'd said he needed me. For the first time in my life, someone depended only on me. I chased away my thoughts and fumbled with the pony's reins, the leather cinched into fist-sized knots.

And behind me, I heard a squeaking of wheels.

I pulled at the knots. I grabbed them with my teeth. An inch of leather came slithering free.

The wheels chattered and creaked. And round a corner, onto the harborfront, came Stumps. He was leaning forward, his hands swinging back and forth, pushing him on. I attacked the knot with more frenzy than ever. Stumps's cart came faster, and faster still. I tore at the leather. And when the knot was almost free, the pony whinnied and stomped away, and all the slack that I'd gained went tight as a bow.

I turned and ran.

Stumps came after me. His hands pushed and pushed. The cart flew along, bouncing over the cobblestones, right at my heels. I turned to my left, into the alley and down the stairs.

Stumps stopped his cart at the top of the steps. "You're trapped," he said, his voice ugly. He put his hands on the ground and raised himself from the cart. His trouser legs flapped loosely as he swung forward and dropped down a step. He grunted and came down another.

There was no sound but that: the thud of his body on the stone, the hush of his leather gloves. I looked down at the water, rippled by cat's-paws, up at the bleak hint of dawn. The alley was too narrow for me to hope to pass him.

"You're done for," said Stumps. "You're finished."

I braced my shoulders against one wall, my feet against the other, and scrambled up like a chimney sweep. Stumps lunged at me, and his hand brushed my heel. But in a moment I was six feet above him, and he gazed at me with his head tilted back. I gloated down; I laughed. And then with dread I saw him stretch his huge arms and flatten one enormous hand on each wall. He came up, even faster than me, grunting with the effort as he shuffled each hand an inch at a time. He swung in the air like a great crawling spider. Bits of loose plaster showered down as his fingers clawed up the walls. And I gained the roof only a moment before him.

His hand gripped the eave. There was a jolt, a thud, as he swung across the space. His other hand clasped the edge of the roof, and he hauled himself up. He was grinning—an evil, grotesque smile.

I turned and raced to the north, over the brewery, over a tavern. He came after me, moving like an ape, swinging from his hands to his stumps. From roof to roof we bounded along, up steep-slanted shingles, past chimneys, round vents where the wind whistled and moaned.

I climbed from one roof to a higher one; I sprinted across a sagging ridge. I ran and jumped, and all the time I heard him coming, like a thumping, pounding engine.

And suddenly I reached the end. I tottered at the very edge of the last building, over a chasm that dropped straight to the ground.

With a grunt and an oath, Stumps came hurling up onto the roof behind me.

He paused there, his body shaking. Then, slowly, he

moved toward me, crawling along the ridge, dragging himself forward. In the shadows and the wind, he looked like a gargoyle come to life.

The roof sloped steeply, on one side to the harbor and on the other to the street, where the overhangs left a gap of six feet to the opposite buildings. Stumps came lurching, slithering closer.

"Got you now," he said in that loathsome, creaky voice. "Going to give you a whipping, boy." He slid forward. "Going to give you a good whipping."

I turned and ran. I raced down the roof, gathering speed, feeling the wind and the salt air, and I launched myself over the gap. The cobblestones flashed by, and there was no sound at all. Then I landed on the other side, on a roof of rusted tin, and clambered up to the ridge. With a thud, Stumps came across the same way. But I wheeled around at the rooftop, went clattering down, and leapt across the gap for a second time.

He cursed me. He sat sprawled across the metal plates and hammered at them with his fist. But already I was moving back along the roofs, back toward the passageway. I was sure to find Mary there, waiting with the ponies.

I scrambled up and down and up again. Each time I rose to a new ridge, the wind pressed against me with a touch as cold and sharp as knives. In the lee of a chimney I took a moment to rest. Breathing hard, hands wrapped round the bricks, I looked back across the street. There was enough brightness in the sky that I could see every hump and break in the roofs. But there was no sign of the legless man.

I had led him farther than I thought. The roofs seemed endless as I plodded along, weary and sore, not once looking back, until I stood again over the tavern, the passageway open before me. The wind gusted and lulled. And in that moment of silence I heard a rasping of breath.

Stumps was behind me.

Chapter 12
A STONE FOR A HEART

With a cry, Stumps flung himself down to the tavern. His hand grabbed at my ankle, and I went sprawling across the slanted roof and tumbled over the edge.

I closed my eyes, waiting for the shock of cold water, for the blackness to close round me. But instead I fell less than a yard before I crashed into the roof of the brewery. And Stumps landed beside me.

He fastened onto my legs and then onto my arms. And we rolled together, over and over, until I lay on my back with my head hanging over the passageway. His hand clutched at my neck; his fingers almost circled my throat. I pushed against him, but I couldn't move him. I gasped for breath as he raised himself to put his whole weight on me—and his nose disappeared. It simply vanished; one moment it was there, sharp as a beak, and the next there was only a black hole in his face. And in the same instant I heard the crack of a pistol.

His hands flew to his face. Again a pistol cracked; the ball roared past my ear. Stumps reared, tumbling sideways and back, cartwheeling right down the roof and over the edge. The water seemed to open for him, to spread apart and drag him down with white-tipped fingers. He didn't bob to the surface. He went into that water, and disappeared.

Below me, two people stepped down to the last stair. There was Mary, with her fists at her mouth. And beside her, hidden below the brim of his hat, with a pistol in each hand, stood Parson Tweed in his black cassock.

"That one won't be rising," he said. "The man had a stone for a heart."

The parson dropped his pistols into his voluminous pockets and helped me down from the roof. He poked at me with his long fingers. "Are you hurt?"

"A bit," I said, touching my neck.

Gently he pulled my hands away. "Nothing time won't heal," he said. "Though I'd venture a guess the bruises will fade before the memory does."

"You saved my life," I told him.

"You may thank Mary for that. It was she who sensed the danger and fetched me here." He pushed back his hat, and his thin face was smiling. "However, we did arrive at a providential moment."

I looked at Mary and tried to see in her eyes a message, a sign of what she'd told the parson. Did he know everything now, all about Stumps and my father?

Together the three of us walked up to the street. The parson's cassock fluttered at his ankles. "And now, my boy," he said, "have you anything you'd like to tell me?"

I shook my head. I would have liked to know how a parson had learned to shoot like a marksman. But I wouldn't ask him that, nor anything else.

He nodded. "And you, Mary? Is there something you should tell me?"

"Nothing I can think of," said she.

"Very well." The parson smiled again and touched us both. "I shouldn't trouble myself about that fellow if I were you. Spare him no pity, for wretches such as he always come to a nasty end."

With that, Parson Tweed turned away. "You'll be going home now, will you? To Galilee?"

"Yes," said Mary.

"Ride carefully, child." His robes whirled round his legs. "The moors may not be safe this morning."

He pulled down the brim of his hat and walked away. The heavy pistols dragged at his cassock, stretching it across his shoulders. Under the robe, the parson was thin as a broomstick.

"Tell him," said Mary. Her voice was a whisper, harsh and forceful. "Go. Ask him to help you."

She pushed my arm, but I didn't move.

"Can't you believe me?" she asked.

"I'm sorry," said I.

Mary sighed. "You'll have to see it for your own self," she said. "But whoever works the puppets, it edn't Parson Tweed."

"I hope you're right," I told her.

We didn't go back to see my father. He would have heard our voices and known we were safe, and it would only bring him despair, I thought, for us to arrive with no means or hope of setting him free. So we mounted the ponies and rode up to the high road. Dawn was coming fast, and the shadows seemed to run beside us as we cantered over the bridge. I paced my pony with Mary's, skirting the moor on the road past the Tombstones.

The clouds of the gathering dawn swept above us in jagged rows. When we climbed through the cut I saw streaks of black rain out in the Channel and a feather of smoke from the villagers' fire. They sat where we'd left them, on the point below the garden.

The Widow's wagon was pulled up on the grass, the horses still in harness. The old woman stood by the seat, in a bonnet of wine-colored cloth. The villagers sat wrapped in tarpaulins, and behind them, on a churning dark sea, the ship glided through cloud banks. She was closer to shore, at times just a cable's length from the surf; one way or the other, her struggle would end within the hour.

"I can't go home," said Mary. "No matter how my uncle reacts, I can't go home just now."

Nor could I. And Simon Mawgan wouldn't be there while the ship was still embayed, I was sure of that. So we crossed the rise above the road and hobbled the ponies there, out of sight of the wreckers. And we lay in the sparse grass, watching the ship beating to windward. The sea was rougher, the waves higher. But she set her courses as the day began to brighten, and churned off to the east, tossing up spray.

With dawn came a shift in the wind. It wasn't much, less than a point, but the smoke of the wreckers' fire no longer blew directly through the garden. It streamed to the west in bubbles black as molten tar.

The ship was at the far end of St. Elmo's Bay when the wind shift nearly caught her aback. She gybed around, circled close to the surf, and came bounding along the shore toward us.

And with her came a horseman, riding like a Fury up the coast road. In a flurry of capes, he grew from a speck to a regal figure on a fine black horse. People turned their heads to watch him but didn't move from their places. He rode up to the fire and, just as the man at the cromlech had done, stepped from the saddle as the horse reared.

"Uncle Simon," said Mary. "What do you suppose he's been doing all this night?"

"Waiting," I said. He'd been huddled in a secret cove by the Northground cape, waiting there with a match and a beacon.

Mary pointed. "He has no lantern with him."

"Then he's hidden it," I said.

"Why?" asked Mary.

I had no answer. Certainly he approached none of the wreckers, and none went to him. But they were too intent on the ship for that. First one, then another, then the whole lot stood up to watch her coming. With the shift in the wind, she was more likely than ever to clear Wrinkle Head.

The fire sputtered. Smoke backed on the flames, then hauled round in a coil before it settled again to its steady stream. Sweeping across the Channel was a line of ragged black clouds. Behind it, the sky was bright as gold.

"Wind's changing," I said.

Mary rose on her elbows, watching the ship. "This time she's out," she said. "This time she's free."

She was right, but only if the wind held steady. Decks streaming water, a silvery wake leaping behind, the ship buried her bow in the waves. I could just see the people on her deck, lines of sailors ready at braces and sheets.

Again the smoke wavered. The stream of it humped and twisted like a snake.

"What's happening to the wind?" I asked.

"It's not the wind," said Mary. "It's the Widow."

The old woman had stepped up on her wagon seat. She straddled the driver, a foot on each side, and poor Simple Tom took hold of her ankles. She raised her hands. She held her palms toward the wind, then spread her arms wide, and wider, until she stood like a cross before the storm. A shriek of wind tore at her dress and her hair. The ship drove toward the point. Only five lengths to go, four lengths to go.

"Blow 'er down!" yelled Caleb Stratton.

The Widow chanted in a keening voice, and the wind came tearing over the sea, flattening the breakers, flinging spray high over the cliffs. It raged round her, taking her scarves and raising them straight above her head. It tore off her bonnet and carried it away in high, soaring circles.

The ship lay almost flat in the water, her courses rubbing the waves. A longboat snapped from its chocks and rolled over the side. Water barrels tumbled after it.

Along the cliff, the wreckers crouched on the ground. They put their hands on the earth; they lowered their heads and hunched their shoulders. And above them the Widow sang. She screeched like a flock of gulls.

The ship passed so close to the point that her main yard scraped on the rocks of Wrinkle Head. But she was past, and she was safe now, and on the instant the wind fell to a breeze. The ship sailed off with her canvas glowing, and a moment later the sounds reached us—the cheers of the men aboard.

It was Caleb Stratton who rose first from the ground. He cursed the ship. He picked up a stone and flung it after her.

"She's out!" he cried. "Free and clear."

The Widow lowered her arms. "It was that boy!" she shrieked. "It was him, the Devil in disguise." She turned slowly around.

"You all knew the boy," cried the Widow. "Once he lived among you." Her gaze swept over the slope, over the garden, over the ground where I lay. She seemed to stare right at me. "And he's here. He's somewhere close by."

I wanted to run then, to flee back to the ponies. But Mary held me down. The Widow made the sign of the evil eye. She spat on the ground between her spread fingers. "It's him, I tell you," she cried, her voice cracked and brittle. "Didn't he come ashore in the very same spot where he drownded all these many years ago?"

The wreckers mumbled quietly. Some crossed themselves with their fingertips.

The Widow hissed like an angry cat. "You saw him! You all saw him! That ship was ours." She pointed at Simon Mawgan. "It's your doing," she cried. "Put him back in the sea. Put him back in the sea that he came from, or you'll rue the day you let him live."

Simon Mawgan, holding the reins of his horse, stood his ground as Caleb Stratton marched toward him. Brandishing his axe, Caleb shouted, "I know where he is! Find the girl, and you've found the boy."

"Touch the girl and I'll kill you," said Simon Mawgan. "Touch a hair on her head and—"

"Why, we wouldn't harm her," said Caleb. "Use her for bait is all. You always get the rat with the prettiest bit o' cheese."

Mawgan stalked across to him. They stood face-to-face, talking in voices too low to hear. Then Caleb stepped back. "Blast you, Mawgan!" he said. "I've got a way with children, I have. It's called a cat-o'-nine-tails, and that will get the truth out of 'im quick enough."

"I'll handle this," said Mawgan.

"See that you do." Caleb took a step back. "I might tell the girl a story the next time I see her. Tell her about her father, maybe, and what happened one night on the Tombstones."

The next moment Caleb Stratton lay sprawled on the ground. Mawgan had flattened him with a blur of fists. "Stay out of it, Stratton!" he roared. "I'll deal with that damned boy in my own way!"

The Widow cackled. She spread her fingers and aimed them like a gun at Simon Mawgan. She swiveled round as he climbed back in the saddle and whipped his horse into a gallop down the road.

"You'll rue the day!" she called after him, and laughed. "The corpse lights will walk along the moor. The dead will sail upon the sea and the men will be of fire!"

He didn't look back. With dust at his heels, he rode off the same way he'd come.

"Let's go," said Mary. "I want to get to Galilee before him."

"We'll have to hurry," I said.

"No." Mary looked at me through a well of tears. "He'll slow down in a minute. His anger passes quickly."

Chapter 13
FOUR TOGETHER

We rode, not to the farm, but straight to the cromlech. It was my idea. "I want to see if he brings a lantern there," I said. In the daylight, it looked like the strange, half-finished home of a mysterious people. The roof alone must have weighed more than a ton, and it seemed barely balanced on the uprights. But a thousand years it had lain there, and thousands more would see it unmoved.

We passed close enough that I could see the running man and his face of horror. Then we crossed the rise and sat on our ponies down in the valley, listening for the sounds of Mawgan's horse.

"He'll see us," I said.

"Maybe," she said. "Maybe not. I really don't care."

In our time together I hadn't seen her like this, her face as grim as the sky. I nudged my pony next to hers. "Do you still believe in the curse?" I asked.

"I don't know," she said. "I don't know what to think anymore."

She looked up at the sky, then down at the ground, and I reached across and took her hand. "Mary," I said. "What happened to your father?"

"He drownded on the Tombstones. He, my mother, my auntie, and Peter. The four of them together."

"On the same night?"

Her lips barely moved. "The four of them together."

"How?" I asked.

Mary had no chance to answer. The sky to the west, over the farm, exploded into a frenzy of rooks. And a cry came to us, a bloodcurdling shriek, then the sounds of the birds—their wings and their rattling voices. The rooks rose in a black cloud of spinning shapes. And the silence that followed was dreadfully still.

"What's happened?" cried Mary.

The birds were circling above us as we rode through the hedgerows and into the farm. They whirled in a huge mass, a circle stretched by the wind, and in pairs or alone they settled on the roofs and the house and the cottage. They made no sounds; they only watched.

We rode past the stable, past the cottage. "Eli!" called Mary. "Eli!"

The stable door stood open. A heap of loose hay lay deep inside, a pitchfork driven into it with just the handle showing. We turned the ponies loose, and they trotted straight to the hay. And we stood in the clearing among the buildings, in an eerie quiet, with the feeling that someone had come and gone a moment before.

We looked in the cottage, and it saddened me to see it. Only one room, and that was bare as a ship's hold —just a rude table, a rickety chair, a bench to sleep on. His brother had amassed a fortune, but Eli had nothing. Mary closed the door.

"It's not like him," she said, "to wander away. He rarely goes beyond the hedgerows anymore."

"Then he must be in the house."

Mary shook her head. "He would never go in there." She led me to the front of the building. "Not once has he been through the door, not once so far as the porch."

"Because your uncle won't let him?" I asked.

"Shhh!" said Mary. "Someone is in there."

The door stood ajar, daylight flooding into darkness. We climbed toward it, and the planks of the porch creaked under our boots. "Eli?" said Mary, little more than a whisper.

I pushed on the handle. The door groaned open. A sticky wetness plucked at my fingers, and I saw the tips stained with fresh, red drops.

"Blood," I said.

Mary gasped. Then she pushed past me and into the house.

It throbbed with a foreboding silence, a strangeness, that feeling again that someone had been there a moment before. The room smelled faintly of tobacco and the odd spice of burnt tinder.

We walked through the house, the kitchen and larder and dining hall. We peered into cupboards and under tables. And we went up the stairs with our hands squeaking from sweat on the railing.

In Simon Mawgan's room was a great four-poster bed hung with luxuriant drapes. The walls were lined with bureaus and tables, their tops covered with basins of delicate china and all manner of brushes and combs. I snatched open the bed curtains, but no one was there. And when I turned from the bed, I thought for a moment that a ghostly face was watching at a window.

"That's Peter," said Mary, coming in behind me.

I stood staring at a painting, at a boy in sailor's dress with a wild sea behind him. He was large as life, or slightly larger, and the paint had faded until he seemed unearthly pale.

Mary touched my arm. "I've heard Uncle Simon talking to that picture. He talks and cries."

"What does he say?"

"I don't hear the words. Only the sounds." She touched the frame. "He loved Peter more than anything. It must have changed him, what happened that night. He's hard now. Hard as brick. As though he built a wall round himself."

"What did happen?" I asked.

"I only know what my uncle has told me. His wife and Peter went with my parents to London. I don't know why; I was only a baby, too young to walk. I was left with Eli."

She led me from the room and down the stairs. "They were all to come back on the packet," she said. "But they found a ship leaving a day early that would take them to Polruan. She was called the *Rose of Sharon*. The men of the

134

village found her embayed. And she was wrecked on the Tombstones."

"With false beacons," I said.

Mary nodded. "And Uncle Simon was there. He saw it all happen: the ship driving onto the Tombstones; the people standing on the deck and climbing the rigging, all of them calling for help. It was just a sound, a wailing; they couldn't hear any particular voice. It took more than an hour for the *Rose of Sharon* to break up. And then the bodies came ashore, three score of bodies tumbled up on the sand."

We passed through the dining room and out the back door. The air felt thick, and the birds all faced south along the ridge of the stable roof. Mary held her skirts above her ankles as we stepped to the grass. "Uncle Simon walked down there, down to the beach, and he found his son and his wife with their arms round each other. He found his brother nearby—my father—with a piece of my mother's dress torn off in his hand. My mother didn't wash ashore for another two days."

Mary sounded terribly sad, but she wasn't crying. She went before me, down the porch to the ground.

"It was the first time," she said, "that they used the false beacons. Uncle Simon says he doesn't remember who lit them. But he still wakes in the dead of night, thrashing in his bed, screaming—" She stopped. Then: "He's here."

"Who?" I asked.

"Uncle Simon."

He came from the shadows of the stable, out into the yard with the riding cape folded over his arm.

Mary ran toward him. "There's been trouble," she said. "Eli's missing."

Mawgan shook out the cape and tossed it over his shoulders.

"We heard a shout," said Mary. "A horrible scream. And there's blood on the door—at the house. Something dreadful has happened."

She put her fist in her mouth and bit down on a finger. Mawgan held her by the shoulders. "What exactly did you hear?" he asked.

"A scream." Mary closed her hands over her ears. "I'm sure it was Eli, and he screamed. He screamed like a rabbit."

"When?"

"Just a few moments ago," said I. "We heard it from the cromlech."

"The cromlech?" said Mawgan.

"Yes." I stared at him boldly. "Where you keep the lanterns."

His eyes blazed. "You went in there?"

"Yes."

"You fool." He ran his hand across his face, wiping sweat from his cheek and his neck. Wherever he touched himself, his fingers left ugly red smears.

"You've blood on your hands," I said.

He turned a palm toward his face and spread the fingers open. He looked at his hand as though he'd never seen it before.

I said, "It was Eli who sent me there."

His face flushed with anger. "Look, boy," he said. "You

don't know what you're doing. You're like a horse with blinkers, going blithely along without seeing what happens around you."

I started to speak, but Mary grabbed Mawgan's arm and stared at his hand. "It *is* blood," she said. "Uncle, what's going on?"

"Eli's dead." Mawgan rubbed his hands together as though he was washing them. "I found him in the stable, in the hay, with a pitchfork through his ribs."

"No," said Mary. She covered her face with her hands, and her body heaved with sobs. "Not Eli. Please, not Eli."

"I'm sorry," he said. And for a moment he held her more closely.

Mary stared up at her uncle, and her lips trembled. "You weren't going to tell me," she said.

"Of course I was."

"You weren't. You wouldn't have said anything if it wasn't for the blood."

"Mary, he was my brother."

"And you *hated* him." She backed away from her uncle. There were fingerprints of blood on her shoulders. "Did you do it?" she asked. "Did you kill him?"

"Mary!"

She bolted. She grabbed up her skirts and ran for the stable. And Mawgan turned to me. "Do you see what you've done?" he said. "Do you?"

"What *I've* done?" I said. "And what happened on the Tombstones the night Peter drowned?"

His eyes were dark and hollow. I wanted to stare him down, but I couldn't. They were huge, frightful whirlpools that spiraled off into nothing. And I looked away, my face burning.

Mawgan laughed. "You're no more a man than the crabs that crawl on the beach," he said. And he raised his hand and knocked me to the ground.

I rolled away, thinking he would kick me. But he only glowered like a man who's come across a beetle in his path. "She's all I've got," he said. "Don't try to deny me that." Then he turned his back and walked off to the house.

I found Mary crouched on the stable floor, pulling handfuls of hay from the pile. Eli's legs poked out, stiff and straight, and his face stared up through the yellow stalks. His eyes were closed, his mouth a wide O. Mary cleared the hay away; she brushed at his chest.

Four holes made a row across his shirt, the cloth puckered and torn, stained with dark blood.

There was hay in his hair, in his collar, in his fists. He looked like a scarecrow dropped there, a scarecrow bleeding and dead.

"It's my fault," said Mary. "If we'd come here instead of going to the cromlech— Oh, John, he couldn't even call for help."

A few pieces of hay clung to his lips, and I plucked them off. I expected a coldness at my fingers, but instead felt warmth. I pressed my hand against his neck.

"Bring water," I said.

Mary looked at me. I said, "He's alive." In the folds of aged skin, I could feel a beating of blood.

Mary laughed. She laughed and she cried, and she

wiped at her face with the backs of her hands. Then she ran to the water trough and came back with a little bucket sloshing full. She dipped her fingers in it, and touched them to Eli's lips.

"More," I said. And we both scooped palmfuls of the water, and let them trickle on his forehead and cheeks. Then his face twitched, and his eyes sprang open.

His arms swung up, pushing at us. A ghastly cry gurgled in his throat, and I saw the stump of his tongue throbbing like a warted toad.

"Eli," said Mary. "Eli, it's me."

She took his hands. She held him and soothed him until he lay flat again, and the blood oozed from his shirt as he breathed.

Simon Mawgan came back. He had a folded blanket in his hand, and he stopped at the stable door to take a shovel from the wall. "Best we do this now," he said. "There's going to be a howl of wind tonight. Rain such as Noah never saw." The shovel clanged like a funeral bell.

Eli opened his eyes but didn't move at all. Mary crouched over him. "He's alive," she said.

"That can't be," said Mawgan. "I pulled the fork from his ribs myself." In four steps he traveled the length of the stable. Then he grunted. "So he is."

But only just. Eli lay white and still, like a huge cocoon. His breath had a wheeze in it, and each rising of his chest pumped new blood from the holes.

"Help me," said Mary.

Simon Mawgan tossed the shovel onto the heap of straw. He knelt down and stretched the blanket from Eli's feet to his neck. He slid his arms underneath and picked up his brother from the floor. "Get a fire going in the cottage," he said to Mary.

"No," she said. "Take him to the house."

Mawgan shuddered. "I think the cottage might be best," he said.

"Uncle, please." She looked up at him, nearly crying. "Please," she said again. "Put him in my bed."

Mawgan did what she asked. He took Eli up in his arms and he carried him, swiftly and easily, out from the stable. And for the first time in his life, Eli passed through the door of his brother's home.

Mawgan put him on the bed as gently as a baby. But with that done, he held his hands out from his sides as though he'd soiled them with dirt. "Listen," he said. "You'll have to keep pressure on those wounds until the bleeding stops." He touched one of his huge hands to Eli's forehead. "And he's got the fever. So keep him covered and light a fire." Then he left the room.

"Is there no doctor?" I asked.

She shook her head. "Not for Eli. There's not a man in Pendennis who would come out here to help him."

The nursing would be Mary's task alone.

Chapter 14
A TERRIFYING DECISION

Simon Mawgan was right about the weather. The glass fell by the minute, and within the hour the sky was covered with clouds as black and ragged as witches' robes. Mary did all she could for Eli; she filled stone jars with hot water and placed them in the bed; she sponged his forehead and moistened his lips. I stoked a fire in the room's little hearth. But still Eli lay shaking and weak.

When the hour had passed, Mawgan came back to the room. He stood in the doorway, puffing on his pipe. He pointed a finger at me. "The packet stops at Polruan tomorrow," he said. "We're leaving here at dawn."

"At dawn?" I asked.

"That's right. The packet comes but once a month. And if you run off again, I'm done with you. Understand?" Then his eyes shifted to Mary. "The bleeding stop?"

"Not quite," she said.

"Have you washed his feet?"

"Uncle, of course I have."

"Yes. Silly of me." Mawgan stepped out to the hall. "Soon as he comes to his senses, you'll want to have him back in the cottage."

When we heard Mawgan walking through the kitchen, Mary got up and moved a kettle onto the fire. She turned to me with a worried frown. "Do you know that whoever did this to Eli was looking for you?"

"Yes." I'd thought the same thing.

"What will you do?" she asked.

"I don't know," said I. "Do you think I should leave on the packet?"

"Is that what you want?" asked Mary.

It was, though I was ashamed to face it. I wanted to get on the packet and go as far and as fast as I could from this place. I was more frightened than I'd ever been, and I wished—I *ached*—that Mary would tell me to go.

But all she said was "Watch him a minute," and left the room.

I could hardly bear the thought of going back to Pendennis, back to that drain full of rats. Someone would wait for me there. The sound of his boots would stalk me down those lonely cobblestoned streets, and then—from a corner, from a doorway—he would leap from the darkness. No, I decided; I couldn't do it. I couldn't possibly do it. I would wait until morning and then go off with Simon Mawgan, over the empty moors, and—

I couldn't do that either. I thought of Mawgan with his hands covered in blood, ready to scrape out a hole and bury his brother with no more thought than he'd give to planting potatoes. Alone on the moor, anything could happen. He could toss me down a mine shaft, then come back to Galilee and say to Mary, "Well, that's the boy gone." And it wouldn't matter how I screamed for help; I would die alone under the ground, swimming in a pit of rain and muck until I could swim no longer.

I shuddered as I thought of this. It was the same fate my father faced, as though it was meant to be. We would die together, miles apart, calling for each other.

Mary came back with a few yards of muslin and a bowl full of oatmeal. She went to the fire and took the lid from the kettle.

I said, "Mary, what should I do?"

"It edn't fair to ask me that." She ladled water into the bowl, and the steam came up, smelling of oats. "You have to do whatever seems best."

"But I don't know what that is."

Mary stirred the oats into a paste. She used her fingers, and they clotted with it. "What would your father tell you to do?"

I could see him in my mind, lying cold and scared in the drain, begging me to help him. But I had no doubt what he would tell me to do. "Go home on the packet," I said.

"Well, is that what you want?" Mary dabbed at her forehead with the back of her hand. "Do you want to be home, and safe, in London?"

I closed my eyes and thought of the city, of its wonderful streets full of carriages and people, its buildings and docks. I saw myself on the bank of the Thames; I breathed the smells and heard the noises. And yes, that was what I wanted. I wanted it badly.

"You shouldn't blame yourself for what's become of your father," said Mary. "Surely he wouldn't want you to lose your life for him." She brought the bowl to the bed. I stood to pull back the covers, and she started laying the poultice over Eli's chest. She talked to me with her head down, busy with her work. "He might die happily if he thought you were home in London, tending to his business."

His business. I thought of this and nearly cried, though for myself or Father I could not say. I didn't want to be a businessman, sitting at a desk and sorting ledgers for all my years to come. But this I would have to do, haunted forever by that last image of my father fettered in the darkness. He had called to me to help him.

Mary patted down the muslin, and the oats welled up between her fingers. She looked sad and solemn. "Oh, John," she said, "I fear for you. If you go back there, you have to go alone."

"Alone?" I asked.

"I can't leave Eli now. Not like this." She wiped her fingers on the edge of the bowl, then spread a towel across the poultice. "Caleb might be waiting for you. The others too. There's the rising tide and the cromlech curse and—"

"I don't believe in that," I said. "It was a story your uncle made up to scare you away."

"I'm not so sure," said Mary.

"Well, I am," said I. "All this time he's been lying to you. He's been plotting and wrecking and—"

144

"Stop it!" cried Mary. And then, in a whisper, "He'll hear you."

We stood in silence then, listening to Simon Mawgan move through the house. His heavy steps came toward us, and then went away again. And I too lowered my voice to a whisper. "I'm going to go," I said. "I have to go."

Mary sighed. "I thought you would." She drew the covers up to Eli's neck and tucked them gently around him. "I know you're very brave."

In truth, I was terrified. But my mind was made up, and I had to go through with it.

"Listen," Mary said. She squeezed my wrist. "There's a file in the stable. On the shelf by the door. There's a hammer there also, and a few other tools." She spoke quickly. Urgently. "Take *my* pony; it's faster, and it will carry you both. But you must not pass a single soul. No one must see you. No one at all."

"And no one will," said I. "Is there a road direct to Pendennis?"

"There is," said Mary. "But not for you. You'll have to go across the moor. The night will be black—no stars to help you. Keep the wind on your cheek, and ride for your life."

"Yes," I said, and stepped toward the door. My legs were wobbly, but they held me. "Well, goodbye, Mary."

Mary nearly laughed. "Not yet," she said, and pulled me back. "You can't ride through Pendennis in the daylight. And Uncle would never let you go off by yourself. You'll have to wait until nightfall. When he goes to bed, then you can slip away."

There were hours to wait. And the waiting was the hardest of all. I thought of Caleb Stratton and the grinning man. I thought of my father chained to the tunnel wall, of the rats that gnawed at his feet. Simon Mawgan kept looming in my mind, friendly one moment, almost vicious the next. *I'll deal with that damned boy in my own way,* he'd said. *You're no more a man than the crabs that crawl on the beach.* The clouds thickened, and the rain came tapping at the window, and every moment I dreaded a little more the coming of night.

Mary tended to Eli with great fondness and care. When he sweated, she cooled him with water and sponge. When he shivered, she drew the blankets tight round him. She kept touching him, her fingers leaving no marks on that skin that seemed older than it was. But as the hours passed, there was no change in the man; he lay not asleep but not awake, and his breath bubbled on his lips.

I sat by the window, willing the sun to hurry on its westing. But behind the clouds, it crawled. The rain grew heavy. It streamed down the pane and rattled on the roof; it flowed from the eaves in a solid sheet. And soon there was a sound out there, deep with sorrow, a moan of lonely voices.

"That's the wind in the cromlech," said Mary. "When it talks like that, the ships come ashore."

We saw nothing of Simon Mawgan until early evening, when he came tramping upstairs to the doorway. "How is he?"

"The same," said Mary.

Mawgan spread his arms across the door. "So do you

think he might hang on long enough for you to make my supper?"

I was left to watch over Eli. His eyes were not quite closed, and I could see the whites like crescent moons. Now and then his fingers twitched, or the muscles tightened in that awful turtle's neck.

The wind whispered and moaned. The house creaked and the rain scratched at the windows. And I sat alone with a dying man, hearing taunting words in the wind. *Never doooo it. Dooomed. You're doooooomed.*

Then Eli's head jerked from the pillow. His eyes popped open, and he stared up with a wild horror at something that wasn't there. And he fell back, slipping again into his eerie sleep.

By the time Mary came in with a tray full of food and steaming tea, the room had darkened. She brought a lamp, and the shadows drew back as she passed, then crept in behind her. Hidden by row after row of jagged clouds, the sun at last was setting.

"Do you hear it?" asked Mary.

"What?"

"The surf."

I hadn't. But I knew then that it had been there all the time, slowly building, slowly gaining in fury. And for a moment I could hear nothing else but the muffled blasts, as though whole navies were trading broadsides out in the Channel.

Mary put down her tray. "Uncle Simon's just sitting by the fire. I think he means to spend the night in his chair."

"How will I get out?" I asked.

"You'll have to wait." She sat down on the bed and passed me a sausage. "But he sleeps like a log."

With the sun down, darkness came soon after. It filled the room as swiftly and coldly as water in a holed ship. And still I had to wait. Eli twitched on the bed. Once he cried out in his sleep, as though caught in a nightmare.

"Mary?" I asked. "Why does your uncle keep Eli out of the house?"

"He doesn't," said Mary. "It's Eli who won't come in."

"Why?"

"I don't know, really." She sponged his forehead and his neck; she fussed at the poultice. "Eli never had a wife or child, and I think he would have liked to raise me himself after the *Rose of Sharon* was wrecked. But he was poor as dirt, and Uncle Simon had so much; it had to be Uncle Simon. Poor Eli sat down and cried the day Uncle Simon took me away. And all I can think is that Eli never forgave him for that."

"But why did your uncle hit him?"

Mary looked at me, then back at Eli. "Uncle Simon has an awful anger inside him," she said. "It comes out against Eli more than anyone. But I think most of all he's angry at himself. I don't know why, but that's what I think."

And that was the last she would say of her uncles. The lamp flickered in the darkness, and I thought again of the moor; I dreaded going out there. Mary told me to sleep, but I couldn't. "Tell me of London," she said, but I couldn't think of anything I hadn't told her before. And so we sat— and Eli wheezed and shook—until Simon Mawgan fell asleep and the sounds of his snoring rasped through the house.

Mary stood up. It was time to go.

From a table she fetched a candle and a tinderbox. "You'll need a light to work by," she said.

My hands were trembling as I took them from her.

"Remember," she said. "Stay off the roads. And watch for yourself, John."

She came round the bed, and I took her hands. I said, "I won't see you again."

"You might. We can never tell."

"Thank you," I said. "For everything."

She hugged me fiercely. "I think Peter must have been like you," she said. Then she stepped back, and she wiped her eyes. "No more talking. If Uncle wakes, it's over."

Mary went before me, holding the lamp at her waist. She'd kept the house dark, and we moved in a pool of light, through the dining hall and into the parlor.

Simon Mawgan was sprawled in a huge chair, his feet splayed on the hearth, hands in his lap. His head rested on his left shoulder, and his jowls quivered as he breathed huge snoring breaths. And we crept right past him with the floorboards crying like mice.

At the door Mary took a coat from its peg and gave it to me. Mawgan breathed and snored. I slipped the candle and tinder into a pocket; then Mary pressed the lamp into my hands. She cupped a palm over the lamp's chimney and warned me with her eyes to guard the flame against the wind. I imagined the glass was vibrating with her uncle's snore.

"Be careful," she said. Then she raised the latch and cracked open the door.

A cold draft came in, wet with rain. Mawgan stirred in his chair; the snoring stopped, then started.

"Godspeed," said Mary, and ushered me out.

Chapter 15
ACROSS THE MOOR

I threw the coat across my shoulders and plunged down into the darkness and the rain. Before I'd even reached the stable, I was wet to the skin. I found the shelf, and on it a file. It was a good one, the teeth so sharp they glinted silver and gray. I took a chisel and a stout hammer. And I put all of these into a leather pouch.

The ponies shied away from the lamp, but Mawgan's black horse whinnied and stomped. So it was used to the light, I thought, to the glow of a lantern. It was eager to go on whatever business a lantern might lead it to. But I took Mary's pony instead, blew out the lamp, and headed off for the village.

I passed through the hedgerows and climbed up on the moor. The wind raged across the open ground, hurling the rain in stinging blasts. I put my head down and urged the pony on.

Like a ship at sea, I used the wind to guide me. From a

trot to a canter to a full gallop, the little pony carried me along. When the house disappeared behind, I rode over an empty land. And I lay along the pony's back, my cheek pressed against its neck, watching the ground rush darkly past its feet.

Faster. Faster still. Hooves barely touched the ground. A single thump, all four at once flinging water, and we bounded over scrub grass and dunes.

And then I was falling.

The pony pitched forward, and I flew over its head, tumbling onto the wet earth. The pony tried to rise but couldn't. It was slipping backward, clawing with one hoof as it vanished into the ground.

A mine shaft. We'd stumbled right on top of it, crashing through the covering of rotted boards. As the pony struggled, the wood broke away like river ice.

I grabbed the reins and wrapped them round my hand. I braced my feet. The pony thrashed at the planks, flinging up splinters that spun off on the wind. Its belly cracked through the wood, and I fell face first. The reins cinched on my fist and pulled me over the slick ground. Then the platform caved in, and with a nearly human cry, the pony fell backward into the hole.

It dragged me right to the edge. I felt the whole weight of the animal tighten for an instant on the end of my arm, then the bridles tore from its head, and it went spinning down into blackness.

And swaying over the hole, dangling from a thong, was my leather pouch full of tools.

It was snagged on a mere spike of wood at the end of a

broken plank. I couldn't reach it no matter how I stretched, and each time I moved, the pouch only swung more violently than before. First the hammer and then the file poked out from the opening. The wind plucked at the pouch; the rain beat against it. And I saw I would lose it all if I waited any longer.

I gathered myself and lunged forward. My fingers scraped on the thong. It slipped off the wood, and the pouch fell. I nearly followed it down as I reached out and caught it. But I lost the hammer and I lost the file, and my heart fell with them. There seemed no point in going on, yet I couldn't go back. So I took the chisel and left the pouch; I drew up my coat collar and trudged off toward Pendennis.

Before long the wind carried with it the smell of the sea. I kept it on my cheek, as Mary had said, and counted my paces. At six hundred and ten, I came to a road.

It was rutted deeply by the wheels of heavy carts. And though Mary had warned me against it, I followed the road toward the southwest. Listening hard for horses or men, I trotted along, splashing in the rain-filled ruts.

Then I came to a crossroad. And I met Tommy Colwyn.

He was shriveled and black. He hung from a gibbet in loops of great chain that tingled and clanged, that whistled with the wind. His arms rose and fell; his hair streamed out in thin, sparse little clumps. He swung and shook, and he swayed toward me with what seemed like a smile—until I saw his lips hanging in shreds like twists of old rope.

I ran past him and turned left at the fork. The rain drove at me in a furious gust that rattled the chains and howled through the links in a voice straight from the grave. And in the clank and creak of metal, I imagined Tommy Colwyn coming down from the gibbet, staggering after me, reaching out with skeleton hands. I couldn't look back. I felt I'd drop dead if I looked behind me. And I ran and I ran, until I topped a rise and saw the village below.

The few lights of Pendennis shone yellow in the harbor water. And dim as stars of the dawn, tiny and haloed by rain, the saints of the church were watching me come.

I left the road and ran straight for the bridge, down to the banks of the little river. The surf was like thunder, rumbling up the valley. And under the huge arch of the bridge, I rested out of the weather. There was an old skiff covered with tarpaulins, and I sat on its gunwale and cried.

The tide was already on the ebb, the swollen river rushing past in eddies and swirls. Beyond the bridge, where the current met the wind, the water piled into steep-sided waves. When I looked away, the bridge and the shore and the stones at my feet all wavered and flowed like the water. I got down on my knees and searched through the stones, picking them up and putting them down, until I found one that fitted well in my hand, that would do for a hammer.

I'd just picked it up when I heard a gunshot, alarmingly close, and another right after. They echoed under the bridge and back and forth up the valley.

A ship in the bay.

Within moments I heard the horses coming. It was as though the riders had been waiting like racers for the sound of the gun. First one and then many went galloping over the bridge above me. Behind them came the wagons, creaking and groaning, gravel crunching under iron-rimmed wheels. Next would come the people, with axes and picks, and with them the dogs that would sniff me out like an otter.

And I was trapped on the wrong side of the swollen river.

The water was too deep and furious for wading. It would take me too long to walk up one bank and down the other. My only chance was the skiff.

I tore at the tarpaulins. The boat was old and clinker-built, the nails dripping rust. Swallows had built their mud-hut nest in the curve of the stem. And there was only one oar. The tow rope was tied around a large rock, the rope so rotten at the end that it was easier to break than untie. But I stuffed the tarpaulins down in the bilge and rocked the boat up on its keel. I waited for a gust. Then, in the roar of wind, I pushed against the boat.

It slid easily, with a rumble of stones that no one would hear. The river caught it and pulled as I pushed. I clambered over the transom and landed in a pool of water.

The boat leaked like a half-shingled roof. Water welled up through the garboard seams and trickled past the transom. But I burrowed under the tarpaulins as I went sweeping out from under the bridge.

If anyone saw me, nobody cared. The old boat rocked and spun down the river, bow first, then stern first. It hit broadside to the waves, shipping a cold gallon of water before it leapt on a crest and twirled end over end.

Water slopped in the other side; the oar floated up and bumped against my knee. I grabbed it and threw off the tarpaulins.

The bridge was well behind me, a black hulk in the rain. A lantern bobbed across it, held by a man who shimmered in its light like a silvery ghost. I knelt on a thwart and paddled with the oar. But the skiff only turned in its place, and the next wave burst against the bow with a crack of old wood.

The current was stronger than the wind. I rolled and crashed through the waves, sweeping down past the first rows of buildings, bailing with my hands as the rain hammered down. And to seaward I heard the breakers, the awful roar of enormous waves.

In the village, windows bright with light blinked to darkness. I went rushing past the chandlery, down the row of roofs where Stumps had chased me. Then the skiff reared up and pitched me back to the stern. And when I reached for a handhold, I found the notch cut in the transom, the U carved out for a sculling oar. I cursed myself; anyone else would have seen it right away.

I swung the oar round and dropped it in the groove. The blade splashed into the water behind me. I heaved and pushed, and the skiff crawled forward. The rain fell with a hissing, steaming violence, flattening the waves. Half full of water, the boat moved like a sponge. But at last it bumped against the seawall just above the brewery, and turned to rub its planks against the stone.

I grabbed at loose brick, at clumps of grass. It all came away in my hands. And then the drain tunnel opened before me, gushing water thick with slime, but I reached up and wedged in my arms. When I stood on the bow, the boat nearly sank under me. I crawled into the drain, through the torrent of runoff, with the tow rope in my hand.

I couldn't see my father, and for a horrible moment I thought he was gone. Then I heard his breathing and I said, "Father, I'm back." And he said, "It's you? Oh, dear God, it's you."

Water raged through the tunnel. It had covered the shelf where Father lay, and now lapped just below it. I hitched the tow rope to a link of chain, and in the darkness I emptied my pockets onto the bricks.

"The tide," said Father. He coughed; even talking was an effort for him. "The tide . . ."

"I know," I said. "It's falling now."

I opened the tinderbox and took out the flint. I held it as though it were gold, so frightened was I that it would fall from my hands and go plinking down to the sea. I struck the flint. Sparks flew like fireflies, settling in the tinder. When it smoldered, I got the candle going. It filled the space with its yellow glow.

My father lay just as I'd left him. He was ghastly pale, and even the faint light of the candle hurt his eyes. Driven by the storm, the tide had risen to his shoulders, leaving only splotches of dry cloth, like islands, on his chest and knees. His foot was —

I couldn't look. The rats had come back.

I covered the chisel with my coat to muffle the sound, and by candlelight I set to work — tapping, tapping on the iron collars around his wrists. He'd pulled at them until the skin was stripped off like a bracelet, and with every strike of the chisel his hand flexed in pain. I hammered and hammered until my hands were numb. Then I lifted the chisel and saw the sad little scratch I'd made in the metal. I hadn't done much more than chip off the rust.

"Is it working?" asked Father.

"Halfway there," I lied.

The sound of my work rang through the chamber. The candle guttered. Black smoke stinking of tallow wafted over us. A chip broke from the stone and ricocheted off the walls. At each blow a tingle shot up my arm.

"Let me see," said Father.

There was a gouge in the metal, a groove no deeper than a ha'penny's width.

Father groaned. "No use," he said. "Never do it."

I didn't answer. I gritted my teeth and raised the stone again. The sound I made was steady as dripping water— *clink-clink, clink-clink* —and Father clenched his fists and trembled, as though each strike of the chisel shook right through him. A corner chipped from the stone, another a moment later. A powdery dust covered my hands and filled my nostrils. It turned to a red mud on Father's wrist. And this was just one collar. One of four.

I sat back against the wall. Father was right; it couldn't be done.

He rolled his face toward me, and I saw he was crying. "You tried," he said. "Did your best." I had to strain to hear him. "Leave me now."

"No!" I said. I snatched up the rock and attacked the

158

collar with a fury, chips of stone flying like snow. Then the stone cracked in two, and my fist drove right down on the chisel. And the sound seemed to echo in the building above us.

But it wasn't an echo. Someone was up there, crossing the floor. Someone was coming toward us.

Chapter 16
A DEAD MAN RISES

The trapdoor cracked open. The candle flame grew in the draft, reaching up, brightening the space. Fingers came through, feeling at the door. Then it banged open, and the candle went out.

There was a gasp from above us. "John! John, it's me."

"Mary," I said. I felt relief, and tremendous joy that she had come to help me.

I fumbled in the dark to find the tinderbox. I could hear Mary coming down through the hatch in a rustle of clothes.

"Light the candle," she said. I knew she was close beside me, but her voice seemed muffled and far away.

I said, "I'm trying."

I struck the flint and got the tinder glowing. And when the candle caught—when I raised my eyes—I was looking straight at Parson Tweed.

He wore his black cassock, but not the hat, and his

head—like a bleached skull—suddenly leapt from the darkness as though it hung suspended in the air.

My hands shook so badly that Parson Tweed had to bring the candle to the flame for me. And only then did I see Mary kneeling at the edge of the door, holding back her rain-soaked hair as she peered down through the hole.

"We've brought another file," she said. "And a handspike."

"Where's your uncle?" I asked.

"I don't know." She slid the spike to the edge of the hole. "We heard the gunshots, and he rode off right away. Eli was sleeping, properly sleeping, so I—"

"She chose to come to me," said the parson. The spike was neither very long nor very heavy, but he had to struggle with it, and he panted. "I must say that I only wish you both had come sooner." He let the spike rest on its tip and leaned it toward me. I took it from him. "Proverbs nineteen: 'A foolish son is the calamity of his father.' It would appear that I've arrived none too soon."

He stood in the rush of water and touched my father's face. He asked him, "Have you been here since the wreck?"

"Yes," said Father.

"Can you walk, do you think?"

"A bit." Father groaned. "My foot—"

"Good heavens!" said Parson Tweed. He blanched at the sight of Father's rat-bitten foot, then looked at me with a scornful frown. He patted Father's hand. "Well, we shall just have to see what we can do."

I went to work with the handspike, not on the metal

collars but on the locks that held them closed. With the spike thrust through the hasp, I pulled and pried.

"Harder," said the parson.

The spike bent like a longbow. The end sprang loose, and I fell back into the cold stream of runoff.

"Again," said Parson Tweed. "Mary, come help him, child."

Mary dropped down through the hatch and into the water. The parson sloshed to the back of the tunnel, by Father's feet. "A good, sharp pull," he said. "That should do the trick."

I fished out the spike and worked it into the hasp. Mary took the handle; I put my hands between hers. "Pull," I said. Mary leaned back, her whole weight on the spike. It bent, twisted, and then the lock sprang open with a crack, sending Mary and me tumbling to the floor.

"Splendid!" said the parson. "Now the next one. Come, come."

The second, the third, went as easily as the first. My father sat up, sprawled like a rag doll against the brick. For nearly three days he'd lain cramped and sore, and he sat now almost laughing, his hands trembling as he pressed them to the wall and filled his palms with trickling rain.

"Still one to go," said Parson Tweed. "Come along. A time for every purpose."

I carried the spike down toward him. The last collar held Father's ankle, the same foot the rats had gnawed. Parson Tweed bent down and slipped the spike through the lock. "Now pull," he said. He slipped his hands in the pockets of his cassock. "The two of you pull."

We put our weight on it. Mary lifted her foot, dragging down on the spike. Father was watching, urging us on with little nods of his head. The lock snapped, and again Mary and I fell to the floor. The spike splashed down between us, hitting my leg with a thump.

"You've done it," said Father. "You've—" Suddenly he stopped.

"Yes," said Parson Tweed. "You've done it now." He stared straight at me.

In each hand he held a pistol.

Mary cried out. "What are you doing?"

"God helps those who help themselves. He sent you here to break these chains because I could not do it alone." The parson aimed the guns right at me. "I went looking for you, boy, up at Galilee. But it was Eli I found in the darkness of the stable, and it's a pity what happened. Still, there's a sense in God's mysterious ways. You were spared so that you might come and help me here."

"You're the one," said Mary. "You're the puppet master."

Parson Tweed frowned, then slowly smiled. "I see," he said. "Yes, they are rather puppetlike, Caleb Stratton and his lot. Heads of wood. Feet of clay."

"But I trusted you."

"Oh, child, this is not for me. It's for the church. For all of Pendennis."

"And Uncle Simon? Is he one of your—"

"Hush now, Mary." His eyes narrowed. "I mean to have that gold. I want to know where it is." He kept his pistols steady, but turned his eyes to Father. "I suspect you've hidden it, hmmm? I suspect even the boy doesn't know where. But you brought it ashore and buried it, most likely somewhere near the Tombstones."

Father didn't speak. He just stared dumbly at Parson Tweed.

"I'll kill the boy!" With his thumbs, the parson cocked both pistols. "As the Lord is my witness, I'll put a ball right through his heart."

"No!" said Father. He held out his hands.

"I don't want to do it," said Parson Tweed. "I have no taste for this sort of thing. If you'll only tell me where the gold is, the three of us shall go down and dig it up together, hmmm? And then you can go. I give you my word on that."

"No!" cried Father again.

"The boy for the gold," said Parson Tweed. He looked right at Father, and said it again: "Come now. The boy for the gold."

"Tell him!" I shouted. For a moment the pistols wavered. They turned away from me, and I snatched up the handspike. I leapt to my feet—and the room exploded. I saw a flash of light blossom from the parson's right hand, saw the flames and the smoke spew from the pistol's barrel. I even saw the ball—or thought I did—hurtling toward me. And Mary was screaming and Father was shouting and the sound of the gun was deafening. I staggered back, sure I'd been shot, not knowing where, reeling and tumbling through the mouth of the drain, falling forever, it seemed, until I broke headfirst through the cold, dark waters of the harbor.

I sank deep. I rose to the surface, kicking and writhing. The blackness of night and the blackness of water were one and the same. Mary's screams stopped in a sudden, rumbling silence, then started again, started and stopped as I breathed first air and then water as I clawed at the stones of the wall. And finally my feet hit something soft, and I kicked against it, rising up with my hands flailing, until at last they found something to cling to.

The skiff. It wallowed at the foot of the steps, almost filled to the gunwales. I got my hands inside, and then my arms, and I rested, with the rain falling coldly on my shoulders.

And up from the gloomy sea, dislodged by my feet, rose the body of Stumps.

He floated on his back like a hideous jellyfish, bloated and pale. The tide bumped him against me, and his hand went round my waist. I pushed him away, but he only came back. The water rippled over his face, sloshing in his mouth. His eyes were round and white as eggs.

Above me, the door to the brewery crashed open. Mary flew out, screaming my name. Only moments had passed, though I felt older by a year.

"John!" she cried. "John!"

I tried to answer, but I couldn't. I saw Parson Tweed stoop through the doorway, still holding one of his pistols, and for an instant our eyes met. Then, with one step, he grabbed hold of Mary's clothes.

She fought him. She struggled and kicked. She tore free, but he only caught her again, wrapping her hair in his fist

166

until he forced her to her knees. Then he raised his pistol and fired.

It was a wild shot. The ball struck the water beside me, raising a geyser that vanished in the wind. He raised the pistol like a club. Up went his arm.

And he crumpled like a hammered nail. He bent forward, sagged, then fell to the stone.

In the doorway behind him, half leaning on the wall, stood my father. The iron spike dropped from his hand.

I pulled myself up the length of the skiff, up to the bow, where it nudged against the steps. Mary came to help. She pulled at my elbow, and I got my knee onto the stem. The skiff went under, and Stumps floated over the gunwale; when it bobbed up again, he was nestled inside. I lifted Parson Tweed by the shoulders, Mary took his feet, and together we heaved him down the steps. He turned a slow somersault and splashed into the skiff beside Stumps. Arm in arm they floated, with the cassock spread across them like a blanket.

I gave the skiff a shove, sending it out into the current. It snubbed against the tow rope, pulled again, and the old rope broke with a twang of spray. Borne by the tide, the boat floated down toward the sea. And in a moment it was lost from sight.

Father was weak, but he could stand. He put an arm round my shoulders, most of his weight on my back, and we hobbled up the steps, through a stream of rain.

"Tell me," he said. "What gold did he mean?"

"From the barrels," I snapped through gritted teeth. I was angry that he would still hide from me the truth of his smuggling, bitterly hurt that he had seemed to choose the gold over me.

"The barrels?" His feet dragged on the stone. I had to stop, and we stood on the second-to-last step, under the shelter of the building.

"I know all about it," I said. "The barrels we loaded at night were half full of sawdust. You were smuggling gold, Father; gold or diamonds. The sawdust gave you away. But it's the only reason that Stumps kept you alive."

My father didn't answer. I could feel him shaking, his breaths going in and out. I thought he was crying; but he was laughing. "Sawdust," he said, and laughed even harder. "He saved me for sawdust. John, put me down. Put me down a moment."

I lowered him to the steps. He sat there, leaning forward, wiping his eyes as he laughed. "There was no gold," he said. "Where on earth did he get that idea?" He laughed again, tears streaming. "All we were doing was buying second-rate wine from a third-rate vintner. And they cheated us, John. Those Spaniards made us load at night, and gave us false-bottomed barrels. I knew it as soon as the sawdust showed up in the pumps."

Mary laughed, too. "They sold you sawdust?"

"For a bargain!" said Father. "And the wreckers thought it was packed full of gold?"

"Yes."

"It shows you, doesn't it." Father pushed himself up. I gave him my shoulder to lean on. "Evil men will always see evil in others," he said.

His words didn't say much for me. I felt rather ashamed

as we went up to the waterfront street. Mary had the pony tied to a post, a saddlebag draped over its back. "It's got food in it," she said. "We'll fetch the other pony and—" She saw my face and stopped. "He's gone, edn't he?"

"A mine shaft," I said. "We broke through the top." Mawgan had warned me of that; I'd thought he meant only to scare me.

Mary bit her lip. "Then you'll have to take this one," she said. "The bag's full of food. You'll have plenty to get to Polruan. Leave him at the stable by the wharfs. Uncle Simon will fetch him back."

"Your uncle will be busy tonight," I said. "He's got a ship to wreck."

"John, please!" cried Mary.

"But the parson." A gust of wind moaned through the village. "You said yourself that your uncle was with him the night they wrecked the *Skye*."

Mary stared at me. She didn't speak.

"He's a wrecker," I said. "This proves it."

"No." Slowly she shook her head. "You're wrong. You must be wrong."

"When you go home . . ."

She lowered her head. "I don't think I'll be going home tonight. Now leave, John. Please hurry."

With an effort, Father straightened. "Young lady," he said, "I'm in your debt. If there's something I can do, anything at all—"

"No," said Mary. "There's nothing I need."

Father smiled. Somehow, though he was wet and shivering, though his clothes were tattered and stank of the cistern, he looked proud and elegant. A gentleman. He clapped a huge hand on my shoulder. "Let's go home," he said.

It seemed impossible: we were finally leaving Pendennis. We stood on the dark street, in the torrent of rain, and grinned at each other like fools. Then I helped Father onto the pony. I started to climb up behind him, but he stopped me. "In front," he said. "You'll do better than I can."

Mary untied the bridle and passed it up. She put her hands on the pony's nose and let it nudge her cheek. "Don't ride him too hard," she said. "He's not as strong as the other one."

I reached down and took her hand. "Mary, I—"

"Hush now." The pony pranced sideways, pulling my hand from Mary's. "I'll miss you," she said. "I'll think of you often."

And then she was gone.

She went at a run, and I watched her. I watched until she was lost in the darkness. Then I felt my father's hands close on my waist. They squeezed me hard. I shook the reins, and we started off for Polruan. The pony seemed to sigh when it passed through the old wall and started up the hill.

I looked back only once, to see the church behind us. The building was dark, foreboding, and the row of saints— unlit—looked like men hiding in the shadows. It was there, I realized, behind the figures, that Parson Tweed had kept his lookout for ships imperiled in the night.

But it seemed lonely now. Empty. As though the saints who'd watched over me were watching no more.

Chapter 17
FALSE BEACONS

I wish that my story ended here. In a small way, it does. For what happened next changed things forever after.

Before we gained the hilltop, the signal came. Three shots in quick succession, they floated across the moors and cliffs, through the valley and the sky. And before the sound had died away, I reined the pony in.

"Why have you stopped?" asked Father.

"That was a signal," I said. "There's a ship out there, and now she's coming ashore."

I turned the pony to face the wind. Its mane lashed against my legs; it tossed up its head. I couldn't see the Channel, but I could hear it—waves dashing in endless rows against the cliffs.

For a while my father sat quietly behind me. Then he touched my arm. "Son," he said, "we have to go."

I twisted around on the pony's back. Father's face was

grimly set. "I can't," I said. "I can't leave here knowing the wreckers are at work."

He held out his hands. "But what can we do? It's best if we bring others," he said. "We can find a magistrate, a—"

"They'd come too late," I said.

"But John, really. What could we possibly do?"

"I don't know," I said. "Maybe nothing. But I can't leave here knowing I didn't try."

Father sighed. "Yes, you're right. You show me for a better man, John."

"No, Father!" I jumped down from the pony and stood with my hands on his knee. "That's not what I meant."

"But it's true."

"You're hurt," I said. "You can hardly walk." I held the reins up toward him. "I want you to go on to Polruan. Will you do that?"

He held down his hand. I laid the reins across it. But instead he took my wrist. "No," he said. "We'll go together. When this business is done, we'll *both* go to Polruan."

He stiffened his arm, and I swung up in front of him. I cried out to the pony and turned it back toward the village. Mud flew from its heels as we raced down the hill, left at the crossroad, into the valley. We hurtled on, hooves drumming on the bridge, rain stinging my face. And when we'd crossed the river, I gave the reins a tug and steered the pony off the road. Father kicked against its ribs, and we headed off at a canter, across the moor to the sea.

We came to the shore east of the Tombstones, at the cliffs that Mawgan had told me were haunted. The surf crashed at the foot of them with a ferocious roar, with a grinding of rocks and a rolling, surging spray. We sat on the poor scared pony and stared at the sea. Far to the south lightning flickered, pale as sparks from a tinder.

And there before us was the ship.

Like a shimmer of mist, faint and indistinct, she looked no bigger than the *Isle of Skye*. Then again the lightning flashed, and it lit her ghostly gray. The enormous hull of a full-rigged ship, towering masts with a stack of yards: She was a giant with a score of men, driven along by the smallest sails, topsails double-reefed.

"Couldn't be more cautious than that," said Father. "They're not at all sure where they are."

"But they're coming in," I said. The masts were nearly in line, the sails overlapping.

Father put a hand to his forehead, shielding his eyes from the rain. "On the *Skye*, we saw lights. But—"

"The wreckers," I said. "When the ship's closer in, they'll light their false beacons."

"So that was it. A light in the shadow of death," said Father, and I shuddered.

We rode slowly toward the Tombstones, on ground that shook with the surf. The wind rushed up the face of the cliffs, and the pony's mane stood in the air like the fur of a frightened cat. The rain fell in sheets, and the sky to the south flared with lightning.

"Look!" said Father.

On the hills above us the villagers were gathering. I saw them come over the rise, carrying their tools of destruction. They seemed to come from the earth and sink below it

again, on foot and on horseback, <u>adults and children. And</u>
then came a wagon huge and black, enormous horses in
the harness. The Widow.

*When the Widow arrives, there's a wreck in the offing. She feels
it like a coming storm.* But the last time, she'd been wrong.

Father grabbed my shoulder. "Look," he said again.

"I see them," said I.

"No. Look there."

Thirty yards before us, in a hollow at the cliffs, stood a
horse with no rider. Empty stirrups twisted and turned; its
tail flew like a streamer. Then it raised its head in a dark
tangle of mane, and I saw it was Mawgan's horse, Mawgan's fine pacer.

With a happy little snort the pony started toward its
stablemate. It swayed under us, carrying us along. Then
suddenly it shrieked. It reared and bolted, and I fell with a
thud to the ground. Father clung to it somehow, grabbing
for the reins, and in a dim flash of lightning I saw what the
pony had seen.

Simon Mawgan crouched at the edge of the cliff. All in
black, from his boots to his hat, he shone in the lightning
glow. Even his face was darkened—a mask of coal dust or
boot blacking. His eyes peered from it as though he was
only that: a pair of eyes in the darkness. He stood still as
death. And on the ground before him was a lantern.

I walked straight to him. The surf thundered and the
rain came down. "I knew I'd find you here," I said. "With
a ship for the wrecking."

He squinted at me as the rain poured from the brim of
his hat. Even his horse seemed to stare at me. Father had

brought the pony under control, and came toward us along the cliffs.

"Your father?" asked Mawgan.

"Yes," said I.

"And Stumps?"

"He's dead."

Mawgan barely flinched. "No shame in that."

"So is Parson Tweed."

"The parson?" said Mawgan. "You killed Parson Tweed?"

"He shot at me," I said. "He was the leader, wasn't he? He was your hoop that held the staves together."

An odd expression came to his eyes. It was a look of surprise, as though the idea had never occurred to him. "And the gold?" he asked.

"There is no gold. Never was."

He chuckled. "If that's the truth, it's the one thing you never lied about. Now, let me get on with this business."

I hit him full in the chest. I drove against him, head down like a ram. We fell together, crashing onto the ground at the very lip of the cliffs. I leapt away and snatched up the lantern.

"Wait!" he shouted.

I hammered my fist against the glass.

"You fool!" said Mawgan. He rolled on the stones and the grass, struggling to his feet. Then Father brought the pony in, and its hooves trampled round him. It was a scene of madness: Mawgan all black on the ground, only his eyes and his hands to be seen, the pony stomping and snorting above him, and Father on its back like a demon.

I bashed at the glass. I raised the lantern and flung it down. The lens shattered. Then I hurled the thing over the cliff—"No!" screamed Mawgan—down to the rocks and the surf far below.

Mawgan lay still. The pony stood over him, straddling him, and he put his hands around its forefoot. "You've doomed them," he said. "You've lost the ship." He sounded wretched, in utter despair.

Father stared down. "What's he talking about?" he asked.

"Look at the glass," cried Mawgan.

There were shards of it at my feet. I knelt down and took one in my hand. It was thick and darkly colored.

"I wasn't going to wreck the ship, you fool. I was going to save it!"

The lightning flared and shone off the glass, and for an instant it glowed a deep blue in my palm.

"The corpse lights, boy," said Mawgan. "*I* am the corpse lights."

Pale blue lights that wander on the beach and the cliffs, Mary had said. *It doesn't matter what's happening; if people see the corpse lights, they run away.*

Mawgan shoved at the pony's hoof. To Father he said, "Sir, would you kindly back this animal off before it sends us both over the edge?"

I nodded to Father. He moved the pony back, and Mawgan sat up. His poor horse still watched us, bewildered.

Mawgan glared at me. "Why do you think I hide the lanterns in that stone heap? Why do you think I ride down here at the sound of the shots?"

I shook my head. I didn't know anymore.

"I walk with the lantern," said Mawgan, "and they see me and think it's the corpse lights. I couldn't help the *Isle of Skye*. Parson Tweed kept me half the night, and now I know why. But tonight . . . tonight I waited in Mary's garden—"

"She told you about her garden?"

"Of course not." He rolled to his knees and stood up. "But who do you think tears out the weeds? Who do you think waters the flowers?"

I said, "She thought it was magic."

So I was wrong, and Eli was wrong. And Mary—poor Mary—had been right all along when she'd told me to trust Simon Mawgan. But now I had thrown away the one hope of saving the ship. "Why?" I said. "Why couldn't you tell me?"

"No one could know," he said. "Not Eli, nor anyone else. Even Mary had to believe in the corpse lights."

The lightning flashed. And for the first time we heard the thunder that followed, the storm coming closer. It was a rolling, sinister sound that shook at the air like fists.

And at that instant, on the hills beyond us, a light flared up from the darkness. The wreckers were lighting the beacons.

A moment later there were two of them burning. We could see in their golden glow the shapes of the men, the ragged clothes of the Widow, two pyramids of oil kegs to fuel the lanterns. And out in the Channel, the ship turned toward the lights.

"She'll touch in less than an hour," said Mawgan. "She'll come aground on the Tombstones, and that will be the end of her." He stood with his back to us, facing the wind and the rain, shouting against the surf. "They might put an anchor out, but it won't save them. They might chop down the masts, but in the end they'll come ashore. They always do."

"You know a lot about it," said Father.

"I've done it!" Mawgan whirled round just as the lightning flared. The blacking on his face was mottled by the rain, and his skin showed through like a skull. "I wrecked the *Rose of Sharon*!"

"The ship your brother was on," I said.

"Yes. My brother and his wife, my own wife, and my son, Peter. Nearly all that I loved were on that ship. And I lit the beacons that brought them ashore."

"You're a monster," said Father.

"I am, sir. Yes, that's just what I am." The lightning flashed over him. "But God knows I've paid for it. I lost my son and my wife and my brother. I turned my other brother, Eli, against me, and he loathes me to this very day. I drove my mother mad. But you've seen that, John, what it did to her."

"No," I said. "I—"

"You have," he said gently.

I couldn't believe it. "Not the Widow," I said.

Mawgan nodded. "Mary doesn't know who she is. The poor woman doesn't know herself who she is. But I live in dread that someone will tell Mary. That Caleb Stratton or Parson Tweed—well, there's one worry gone. It's not for any love of me that Eli hasn't shown her the truth. He and all the others, they hold it over my head like an axe."

Father looked down from the pony. "I've met that young woman," he said. "And I believe she would forgive you if you gave her that chance."

The beacons flared and smoked. The rain swirled through the light in sheets of yellow and red. The great ship kept coming.

Mawgan said, "There's only one chance. I'll ride back for another lantern."

"No time," I said.

He whistled, and the horse came over. Mawgan collected the reins. "John," he said, "there are fifty men up there on the moor. We've no hope of stopping them any other way."

"And Mary's waiting down at the Tombstones."

"What?" He wedged his boot in the stirrup.

"She's going to try to swim to the wreck," I told him.

"Then there mustn't be a wreck." Mawgan climbed up into the saddle. "Somehow we'll stop them." Then he shook the reins, but I reached up and grabbed them.

I said, "There's a lantern on the porch. We left one there."

He didn't answer. He wrenched the reins from me and beat at the horse with his hat. And he flew off at a gallop toward Galilee.

I stood beside the pony. I touched my father's leg and felt the warmth of blood soaking through his boot. We watched the ship come on, rolling through the swells. The lightning flashed, and flashed again, and the thunder rumbled like enormous barrels. And off to the west, toward the Tombstones, we saw a little boat.

It came round the headland, carried out by the tide into the breakers. We saw it in the lightning and lost it in the darkness, flashes of it now tumbled in a wave, now flung to the crest, a little boat with a man propped on the gunwale. The man never moved at all, but his arm flailed as the boat heaved and wallowed in the waves. It shot straight up, then fell at his side, then pointed toward us; and the boat— filled with water—sailed on along the shore.

The whole sky went white with lightning. The pony trembled.

"Stumps," I said.

It was my little boat, the one from the bridge, and it was Stumps who sat within it, his body lodged in place. He rode the seas with dead, blind eyes, one arm waving as the breakers hurled him about.

"John," said Father, and I looked away from that boat and its horrid crew. "If we're to do something," he said, "we'd best do it now."

The ship drove steadily on. Even in the darkness I could see her then, the water frothing on her decks, the sails so high above them. The beacons burned upon the hills, and I heard a moan of voices.

"We've only moments left," said Father.

The men who guarded the beacons would have pistols and knives, axes and picks. We had nothing. There would be many of them, and only two of us. It wasn't too late to ride back the way we'd come, and straight on to Polruan. It would be easy to do that.

Then I looked at the ship. She bore down on the shore with a bone in her teeth, rising at the head as each wave overtook her, as though she strained for a sight of the land. Very soon the ship would reach the breakers—too late then to turn away.

"I'll go on foot," I said. "Father, do you think—"

"Just tell me what to do."

It was hard to give him orders. I blushed in the night.

"Tell me," he said.

I pointed to the east. "Ride back along the road until you come to a wagon track. Follow the high ground toward the sea and you'll be right above the Tombstones. Wait for me there. I'll try to get to the beacons. But you'll have to—" I couldn't go on.

"I'll have to draw them away," said Father.

I licked my lips. "Yes."

"All right," he said. He clasped my hand. "Bless you, John."

I loped off along the cliffs. The pony's hooves squelched on the grass, then vanished in the boom of surf. And I was alone.

The ship came surging on. I was racing it, running with no inkling of what would happen, thinking only of the men aboard her, of Mary. I remembered her words: *I don't think I'll be going home tonight.* Ever, she'd meant. She would be waiting somewhere at the edge of the sea.

I crossed the slope and circled round behind the lights, one on the ground and one on the back of a pony. When I was right above them, and the ship was coming straight toward me, I stopped and caught my breath. The cliff edge was not far from my left, and the spray of the breaking waves flew above me in the wind. I could smell the fumes of the lanterns; I saw the shadowed forms of the men who tended them, two in capes beside the pony, one more below. He stood and stretched, looking down toward the ship. The lightning flashed, very close, and the thunder came soon after. The ship rode up on a wave, and the water broke round her.

I could hear the wreckers' voices, low and furtive, as they led the pony a foot or two to one side. On the ship, the helmsmen would think they had gone off course. And I watched her masts step apart as she fell off a bit before the wind.

A man laughed. "Like leading sheep to slaughter, ain't it?" he said. He patted the pony's neck.

The other man used the animal for shelter as the wind moaned up from the sea. "Soon now," he said. "Just a brace o' shakes, Jeremy Haines."

Caleb Stratton. I felt cold prickles on the back of my neck, ice in my stomach and heart. Caleb himself, and the grinning man, were tending the upper beacon.

"Who's below us?" asked Caleb.

"Spots."

Shining like a specter, Spots stood in the full glow of the light. He was taking a keg from the pyramid at his side.

"Blast him," said Caleb. "A bit o' baggywrinkle's got more sense than Spots. Run down there and tell him to stand away from the light."

I dropped to a crouch and crept forward. But Spots stepped with his keg back into darkness.

"He's fetching fuel for t'other lantern," said the grinning man.

Caleb grunted. "Then stay where you are."

Lightning streaked again, a flash that turned the night to day. And Spots screamed. "Look there!" he said. "Oh, Lordy, look there!"

"Stow it!" shouted Caleb.

"It's Stumps. He's dead and he's come back. And he has his legs again!"

In the next glare of lightning I saw it myself. The boat below me, filled to the gunwales, Stumps in his place with his arm tossed high. And he did have legs, or he seemed to. He lay right atop Parson Tweed, half wrapped in the black cassock. The parson's legs poked down where Stumps's should have been.

Thunder welled around us.

"You seen it!" cried Spots. "That time you seen it yourself. He's waving at me, Caleb."

There was more than a murmur of voices. And above them rose the Widow's, shrieking as she'd shrieked before: "The dead will sail upon the seas, and the men will be of fire."

"Damn the lot of you!" yelled Caleb. "You're a flock of old hens, squawking at nothing."

Lightning and thunder came together. In the glare I saw Stumps with his new legs kicking. I saw the ship, sails aglow, rushing toward us. And I could wait no longer.

Chapter 18
MEN OF FIRE

I rose to my feet and hurried down the slope. The wind plucked at me; the rain fell through the light of the beacon like a long golden sword. The pony whinnied, and Jeremy Haines turned around. His mouth fell open.

"The boy," he said.

Caleb Stratton swiveled his head, black hair flowing. Behind him, the ship was still coming on.

"Put out that light," I said.

Caleb laughed. "Hear that, Jeremy? The boy says to put out the light." Then his hands moved, digging under his cape, and a pistol barrel glinted in his hand.

I ran past him down the slope, through the shaft of light. It flashed across me, and Caleb raised his pistol. "You're stinking slime," he said. And he fired.

I threw myself down the hill. I landed on my shoulder and flipped forward over the ground. I crashed against Spots's spread legs and saw his oil keg go hurtling over the cliff. Something spun from my pocket—the glass tube I'd taken so long ago from Simon Mawgan, the phosphorus match. I snatched it up and tucked it between my lips.

The sky glowed with lightning, darkened and glowed. Thunder cracked across the clouds; the storm was nearly past. But in the lightning I saw the men coming, the wreckers, Jeremy Haines ahead of them all with the wicked long knife in his hands.

And a man shouted, his voice high with fear: "The corpse lights! God save us; the corpse lights!"

In the darkness of the moor, a bluish light bobbed and danced. Slowly it slid along, rising up and dipping low, twirling over the haunted ground where the seamen lay. I knew it was Mawgan; I knew it was he. But still the hair prickled on my neck.

The wreckers watched in a silence I could feel. Even the surf seemed to fade away as every man and every soul stood to watch the corpse light. Then first one turned to flee, then a second and a third, and others after that. Spots scrambled up and raced away. Wagons creaked and horses cried.

But Jeremy Haines came stalking toward me, straight down the shaft of light. Another pistol appeared from Caleb's cape, metal shining in the beacon. I darted to the pyramid of kegs; I took one in my hands. I held it up to throw it, and Caleb's pistol flared.

The ball crashed through the keg, spilling thick oil down my arms and over my shoulders. The wind sprayed it across the grass, up the slope, and over the barrels where Caleb stood.

Jeremy Haines lunged for me. I brought the keg back and heaved it toward him. I saw him raise his arm, his cape coming up and fluttering in the wind, the light shining through it like the wing of a bat. The keg cracked against his arm, the thin staves caving in. From head to toe, he glistened with oil.

I took the match and held it up. I could hear my father shouting, and saw him from the corner of my eye flitting on the pony across the high ground, driving the wreckers before him. But I didn't turn away; I was watching Jeremy Haines, and he knew at once what I had in my fingers.

"No!" he cried.

I snapped open the match. The paper burst into a white-hot ball. I flung it down on the stack of kegs.

The spilled oil burst into flames. The fire spread in a wild rage, engulfing the pyramid, licking out over the grass, rising in the wind. The kegs exploded in a roaring, searing flash of light.

Jeremy screamed. I could hear his clothing burn, see his outline, bright and orange in the rain.

The fire raged, roaring above the sound of the surf. Half blinded by the glare, I saw Caleb Stratton also outlined in flames. He and Jeremy Haines went spinning across the ground, beating with their arms at the fire that engulfed them. Jeremy Haines reached the cliff and teetered there; then, with a last scream that I will never in all my years forget, he toppled over the edge and into the sea.

Caleb Stratton followed him. For a moment he stood at the edge. Then a roiling smoke wrapped round him, and when it cleared, he was gone.

Father came up on the pony. He dropped straight to the ground and took me in his arms. "It's over," he said. "It's over." And he turned me toward the sea, and bade me to look.

The ship had steered away, bearing up toward the wind with the yards braced fully back. The jibs, as we watched, fluttered up the stays and filled with wind. And she went crashing off across the waves, a beautiful and wonderful thing, tacking free toward the Channel.

We stood and watched, and I let him put his weight on me. "Let's go home," I said.

I spent just one more night at Galilee. We sat in the kitchen, all huddled close to the cooking stove. I'd asked that a fire not be set in the great stone hearth; I'd seen enough of flames.

In his upstairs room, Eli snored softly. Twice every hour Mawgan went up to see him. "Soon as he wakes," he said, "I'll tell him that the wrecking's done. That will bring the wretch round."

"Is it really finished?" asked Mary.

"Yes, child," said Mawgan. He put his hand on her shoulder. "Oh, the ships will still come ashore of themselves. And when they do, we'll get what the sea tosses up. But the killing, the drowning, that's over forever."

Mary had kept her word. She had waited down at the Tombstones, ready to swim to the wreck. It was there we had found her, quietly crying in the rain.

In the kitchen at Galilee, we told her all that had happened, each taking a round of the story, leaving out nothing except any mention of the *Rose of Sharon*. Mary listened to it all, and then turned to her uncle and asked, "Why couldn't you tell me you were the corpse lights?"

"I'm sorry," said Mawgan. "But if you weren't afraid of them, people would start to wonder."

"So you kept it a secret."

"I keep many secrets," said Mawgan, and abruptly changed the subject. "You, sir," he said to Father.

My father looked up from his seat closest to the stove. His foot, bundled thickly with muslin, was propped up on a seaman's chest.

"You'll be careful to keep the bandages clean?" asked Mawgan. " 'Course you will. And stay off that foot, you hear? Young John will fetch and carry for you."

"Oh, no, he won't," said Father. "He'll be too busy for that. It's straight down to business for John."

"Yes," I said glumly. "The ledgers."

"Hang the ledgers!" cried Father. "You've got sailing to learn."

I looked at him, and he was smiling. "Do you mean that?" I asked.

Father nodded. "You've earned it, John. But you can go to sea on only two conditions."

"Anything," I said.

He laughed. "You'll have to apprentice on one of my ships, and—"

"Of course!" I said.

"And eventually command it."

I didn't know what to say. Mary smiled at me warmly, and Mawgan too, through a cloud of his pipe smoke. Then he stood up and clapped his hands. "Well, who's for starry-gazy?"

"Not me," said I.

Father asked, "What's starry-gazy?"

"Londoners!" roared Mawgan. "Sometimes I think you're all as wet as scrubbers."

Father ate his share of that awful pie. He ate more than his share. And he sat up late, smoking pipes with Mawgan, talking of taxes and duties and I don't know what else; I fell asleep in my chair as the voices droned round me.

And in four days I was home.

We came into London on the packet, ghosting up the Thames on the rising tide. It was good to be back, and Father and I sat together on the capstan, watching the north bank go gliding past. Shadwell Dock slipped astern, then Pelican Stairs as we floated up toward the headland.

"He's a good man," said Father suddenly. "Simon Mawgan, I mean."

"Yes, he is," I said.

"He's going to take Eli in. Did he tell you that?"

"No," I said.

"The upstairs room, that will be Eli's, if the poor soul will accept it."

"I'm sure he will," said I.

The packet turned sluggishly, sails hanging slack, and drifted on toward Execution Dock. I said, "Do you think he'll tell Mary the truth?"

Father shrugged. "Simon Mawgan is haunted by his secrets. I imagine that sooner or later he will have to tell her what he's done."

"What will she think of him then?"

"The same," he said. "If she loves him, just the same."

We passed New Crane Stairs, where New Gravel Lane came to the river. It was a street full of taverns, from the Ship and the Queen's Head right up to the Horse and Dray. They were the haunts of seafaring men. Men like myself.

I said, "I love you, Father."

And this is how it ended. I don't know what happened to Mary and Simon Mawgan. I don't know what became of the Widow.

But I do know this. The storms still thrash at the coast of Cornwall. The waves eat at the rock with a pounding of surf and spray. Never again will a sailor look up from a storm-tossed deck and see the false beacons gutter and burn. The wreckers only sit and wait. But on the darkest, wildest nights—or so the story goes—the corpse lights still walk on the beach at the Tombstones.

AUTHOR'S NOTE

There is no doubt that there were wreckers once, men who profited by the plundering of unfortunate ships. Stories of this are found not only in Cornwall, but all along the coast of southeast England, and up and down the eastern shore of North America, from Newfoundland to the Florida Keys.

In the late eighteenth century, Parson Troutbeck of Cornwall's Scilly Islands included in his prayers one that is often quoted in the stories of the wreckers: "We pray Thee, O Lord, not that wrecks should happen, but that if wrecks do happen, Thou wilt guide them into the Scilly Isles, for the benefit of the poor inhabitants."

Other parsons in other places prayed for this same thing. And whenever a ship came ashore, it was a race to be first at the scene. But this was wrecking in its passive sense, as merely salvaging, and it still goes on today. I myself have combed the beaches for shoes and hockey gloves and camera cases when cargo containers were lost from ships at sea. And once, just below my home, a pallet full of coffee, soap, cigarettes, and beer fell from a ship loading at the dock. For days afterward, the harbor was full of little boats as people went searching through the tide pools, armed with dip nets to collect the plunder.

But the violent form of wrecking, as performed in this

story by the men of Pendennis, is a different matter. References to the deliberate destruction of ships can be found in books written as long ago as 1775. In 1882 Frederic W. Farrar wrote in his *Early Days of Christianity*, "The men of Cornwall went straight from church to light their beacon fires."

It is hard now to separate truth from fiction. There are some historians who say that no ship was ever deliberately wrecked, though this is probably going too far. Inside the old clipper ship *Cutty Sark*, now in permanent drydock in Greenwich, is the figurehead from the *Wilberforce*, a ship built in the Bahamas in 1816. A plaque below the figurehead offers this history of its ship: "She was lured ashore by wreckers at Lee, North Devon, on 23rd October 1842. Seven seamen were drowned. (The wreckers tied a lantern to the tail of a donkey on the beach which produced a movement similar to the light of a ship at anchor.) This was the last known instance of a ship being trapped by wreckers."

The history of wrecking as given in this story by Mary to John follows the most popular view. The practice gradually got worse and worse, until harsher laws and penalties ended it altogether.

In any case, it should be remembered that far more imperiled seamen were saved by Cornishmen and others than ever were drowned by wreckers.

For other views, readers may enjoy Daphne Du Maurier's 1936 novel *Jamaica Inn* and the 1974 nonfiction book *Shipwreck*, which contains many photographs of old wrecks and has a text by John Fowles.

ACKNOWLEDGMENTS

When I was a child, my father read me bedtime stories. He gave the people voices: a creepy one for old blind Pew; a roaring one for Billy Bones. He brought the books to life in a way I both loved and hated, for I recall nightmares of pirate ships and smugglers. I saw the *Hispaniola* come tacking up the river that flowed behind our house, two thousand miles from any ocean, sailing all that way to plunder from the pennies that I'd saved in a little metal bank shaped like an Idaho potato. It was somewhere in my father's stories, or the footnotes to his stories, that I first heard of the men called wreckers, who worked at night on lonely shores. And years later, when I set out to write a story that I hoped would be very much like those of my childhood, it was the wreckers I remembered.

My father inspired this story, then helped with research I could not do myself, living in a remote place on a northern island. He dragged my poor mother over half of Cornwall, looking for the haunts of the wreckers. He searched through old books and sent me information by the boxful. He told me of the time from his own childhood when he went inside a cromlech and saw it glowing in the darkness. And finally, he read my story in its various versions, pointing out its errors.

My agent, Jane Jordan Browne, spent years with the

wreckers, always giving me encouragement in the form of little notes: "Don't give up"; "We'll get there yet." Her assistant, Katy Holmgren, helped immeasurably with a major revision as the story came closer and closer to the ones I remembered.

My thanks go as well to editor Lauri Hornik, who led me the rest of the way, through rewrites and copyediting, with many insightful suggestions.

To these people I give much of the credit for what I like about this story, while accepting the responsibility for any faults that remain.

Others who helped include my brother Donald, Kathleen Larkin and the other researchers of the Prince Rupert Library, and—perhaps most of all—Kristin Miller, with whom I live in a house too small. She made it possible for me to stay at home and write. She listened endlessly to the classical music that I play too loudly when I work, and if I sometimes found her wearing earplugs when I took her a section of pages for proofreading, she seldom complained, even when she had hardly seen me for days at a time.

John Spencer's adventures continue
in *The Smugglers*.
Turn the page for a sample chapter
from that exciting companion novel.

0-385-32663-7

Delacorte Press

Excerpt from *The Smugglers* by Iain Lawrence
Copyright © 1999 by Iain Lawrence

Published by Delacorte Press
a division of Random House, Inc.
1540 Broadway, New York, New York 10036

Chapter 1
THE HIGHWAYMAN

We raced across Kent in a coach-and-four, from London toward the sea. Over moonlit meadows and down forest roads as black as chimneys, we took a serpentine route through every little village. I and my father, and a man who never spoke.

"We're going miles from our way on this roundabout route," said Father, bouncing beside me. "I knew we should have stayed the night at Canterbury. I should have stuck to my guns."

"But I want to see this ship of yours," I said.

Father laughed. "Now, now. It isn't mine yet."

Father was a merchant, a landsman. He never thought of a ship as anything but "it." Once he had said, "What's a ship but a pile of wood and nails? Knock it together a different way, and you've built yourself a house."

"But what is she?" I now asked. "A brig? A barquentine?"

Father sighed. He held his cane across his lap, twisting it in his hands. "I believe it's a schooner. And it's painted black, if that helps."

In the moonlight his face was pale, and he seemed to shiver as the coach clattered onto a bridge just beyond Alkham. "It lies to an anchor," said he, "in the River Stour."

"Does she have topsails?" I asked.

"Topsails?" said Father. "Oh, I daresay it does. And an enormous great figurehead, too."

The coach rattled over the hump of the bridge like a box full of pegs. I heard a shout from the driver, and then the crack of his whip, and we swayed round a corner with the axles screeching. On the opposite seat our silent stranger slept, as he had all the way from Canterbury.

He was a gentleman, but a tiny one. Carefully combed, polished and shined, he looked like a doll that a child had dressed in gray clothes and propped there in the carriage. Though Father had to slouch to keep his head from touching the roof, the gentleman sat bolt upright in his tall beaver hat, his little feet side by side on a box of wood and leather. Mile after mile, he had not moved so much as a finger.

I continued my questioning. "What's she called? Does she have a name?"

"Of course it does, John," said Father. "I'm told it's called the *Dragon*."

The gentleman nearly jumped from his seat. "The *Dragon*?" he whispered. "Is it the *Dragon* you said?"

Father stared at him, astonished. "And what concern is that of yours?" he asked. "State your business, sir."

"You're in the trade, then?" said the gentleman. He glanced toward the window.

"Speak up!" said Father, leaning forward. "What trade?"

"The free trade." He covered his mouth and whispered through his fingers. "The smuggling."

"Confound you," said Father. "Who are you, sir?" If the carriage were bigger, he would have stood in it; he would have strutted through it, as he did through his office in London. "What's your name?" he demanded.

"Larson," said the gentleman. He looked to either side. "I'm . . . connected . . . with the trade."

"Then you should be hanged," said Father. He threw himself back against the seat, rapping his palm with his cane. "I'd do it myself; I gladly would."

Larson's hands went back to his lap. His feet, like small animals, made themselves comfortable on the top of his box. Then his eyes closed, and it was as though he had never moved at all. The carriage swept down a long hill, and the hooves of the horses thundered ahead. With a cry from the driver and a jangle of harness, we hurtled down into a forest of beech trees, and the moonlight vanished from the coach. But in the last flicker through the branches, I saw the gentleman smile.

"A word of advice," said he. "You stay clear of that ship. The *Dragon*."

I heard Father snort, a sound I knew well. I had seen his clerks cringe at that noise, whole rows of them turning their heads.

"She's bad luck," Larson continued. "No, she's worse than that. She's evil."

"How can a ship be evil?" I asked.

"I don't know," said he. "I'm only aware of the one that is."

The whip cracked and cracked again. The driver's shouts came quickly, shrill in the clatter of iron and wood. The horses, snorting, pulled us at a gallop, and black on black the trees went by. I could only imagine the speed, but it must have been at least ten miles an hour.

"A ship can't be evil," said Father. "That's nonsense."

"I hope so," said Larson, his voice nearly lost in the clamor. "At least I've warned you."

"And who are you to warn me?"

But Larson had no chance to answer. The horses screamed in sudden fright, and the carriage jolted heavily. I was thrown forward, nearly from my seat. Father's cane went spinning from his hands.

"What the devil?" said he.

A pistol shot exploded, cracking through the night. The carriage skittered sideways at such a speed that it tilted up on two wheels before falling flat again with a jarring bang of wood. As we came to a stop a second shot rang out, and in its echo cried a voice, taut with peril. "Stand and deliver!"

"Oh, Lord," said Father. "A highwayman."

In the darkness we could hear his boots tapping on the road. He came toward us step by step, and when he halted there was silence, a dreadful stillness I could feel. The moon shone through the trees with a light that was cold and flat, more awful than the darkness. It spilled in through the windows and made grim, white ghosts of Father and Larson.

And into that silent, eerie world fell a single sound, the cocking of a pistol.

Father touched my knee. "Whatever happens, John," he said, "you keep your tongue in your head. Understand?"

I nodded; I felt I couldn't speak if I wanted to. Father's fingers squeezed, then fell away. He said, "Perhaps it's the baggage he's after."

"I rather hope so," said Larson. He moved his feet from the box and bent forward to lift it to his lap. The highwayman came closer, the sound of his boots like the sound of the box's latches as Larson thumbed them open. "But I'm afraid it might be myself he wants."

"Driver, step down," said the highwayman. "Quickly now."

The coach rocked. There was a squeal of springs and the thud of heavy boots. A horse stomped and whinnied, and all the sounds of the forest returned, echoing through the trees.

Larson opened his box, and in the silvery glow of the moon I saw a pair of fancy dueling pistols nested there, a gleam of gold and polished wood. They were long-barreled, wicked in their beauty—the most sinister things I had ever seen.

Father stared at him. "Who *are* you?" he asked.

The little gentleman smiled. His hands shook very slightly as he took the pistols from his box. "I think I'm a dead man," he said. "Now or later, I'm a goner."

The harness jingled. A horse whinnied nervously. "Steady there, girl," said the driver softly, and the highwayman shouted, "Come out from the carriage!"

Father went first, with a last glance at me. Larson started

after him, and as he leaned past me he said in a voice so faint I could hardly hear, "The other side. The roof." He slipped a pistol into my hand. His voice was little more than a breath. "If it goes poorly for us, shoot him down like a dog." He slid to the door, and as he stooped to go through I saw the other pistol twinkle behind him, then vanish into the tails of his coat. He was a mysterious man, furtive as a spy, and I had no idea who he was or what he hoped to be. He went down the step with his hand on the brim of his beaver, down to the road beside Father.

I did as he said and went out through the opposite door. I climbed up to the roof of the carriage, and I crouched there among the boxes and the baggage. Below me, in a line, stood the driver, Father, and Larson. The highwayman stayed by the horses, lurking in their shadows.

He was a tall man in a flowing coat of a bright and fiery red. Bandoliers crossed his chest, and into them were stuffed half a score of pistols. He had others in his belt, and one in each hand. He bristled with pistols. His collars were turned up high, and he wore a flat and wide-brimmed hat that hid his face completely.

"A pretty poor turnout," he said. "A pretty poor one, indeed." He took a step forward—he swaggered, really— and stopped by the front of the coach. "Well, turn out your pockets," he said. "Show me the linings." Then, "Hop to it!" he shouted, and laughed. He shoved a pistol in the air and fired, and the flames shot up like a Roman candle. The horses, frightened, clanged against their harness.

"Watches, rings," said the highwayman. "Empty your purses and your pockets. I want to hear silver jingle. Silver and gold." He whirled on his heels and blasted another shot into the forest, then whirled back around as his hands, fast as a juggler's, replaced the pistols with new ones.

"Driver," he said. "What cargo?"

"Nothing," said the driver in a small and frightened voice. "The night coach don't carry no freight on account of—" He trembled, his cap in his hand. "Of the highwaymen, see."

"Well, that's ironical," said the highwayman. "Lord love me, that's rich." He laughed, and I thought then that the man was quite insane. He looked like a pirate in his big red coat, weighted down with enough pistols for a whole band of brigands. But he bowed and straightened, his sleeves billowing, and suddenly he seemed as harmless as a robin hopping on the road.

It was Larson who spoke. "There's nothing for you here," he said.

The highwayman took a step toward Larson. "And who made you foreman of the jury?" he asked.

Larson didn't move. His feet astride a little pile of jewels and coins, he faced the highwayman and said, "Let us pass, and we'll say no more about it."

The highwayman stepped slowly toward him, and even the horses turned their heads to watch. I lifted my hand. The pistol was light, yet it shook in my fist so badly that I had to brace my arm on the baggage rail.

Below me, the highwayman stopped a mere yard from Larson, towering above him. "Well, well," he said. "A little fancy gent. You'd think he just stepped down from a cuckoo clock."

Larson was in the middle, my father to his left, the driver to his right. He looked almost like a child between them. His hands went slowly, smoothly, around his back to his waist, toward the pistol at his belt.

"Look at him," said the highwayman to Father. "A proper dandy, isn't he? A bug in a hat."

"What do you want?" said Father. "You've got our money. You've got my watch." He nudged it with his cane. "Isn't that enough?"

"I think there's more," said the highwayman. "Driver, is there something else?"

"Something else?" asked the driver. He was terrified, I could see; he was shaking head to toe.

The highwayman stretched out his arm and set the muzzle of a pistol against the driver's heart. On the instant, the poor man seemed to crumble. He blurted out, "The boy! There's a boy in the carriage."

I stared down the long barrel of my pistol, and the beaded sight shivered across the highwayman's hat. With my thumb I drew back the flintlock. It snapped into place. That tiny sound, the merest click, seemed to me as loud as cannons. The highwayman spun toward the carriage door. Larson reached for the pistol at his waist, and Father—not knowing it was there—threw himself toward the highwayman. I saw a blur of red; I pulled the trigger. And at the same instant the highwayman's pistol flared and smoked; I watched him shoot my father.

It all happened in the blink of an eye, yet it lasted forever. In the glare from my own pistol, I saw the highwayman's finger squeeze the trigger. I watched the hammer fall, the powder flash. I saw the flames come bright as sunlight from the barrel.

Father staggered back. His cane fell to the ground and his hands clutched at his heart. Then his legs buckled under him, and he dropped in a heap to the road.

It was all madness and confusion. The highwayman turned and ran; Larson fired after him. Then a huge black horse reared up from the forest and thundered past the carriage, the highwayman clinging to its back like an enormous crimson lizard. And it was only then that I really heard the noise of this one long moment. It rushed over me with the smell of powder—the shots, the shouts, the pounding of that great black beast's hooves. It roared inside my head, a din that nearly deafened me.